# WE ARE THE ANTS

# THE SCHOOL FOR
# INVISIBLE BOYS

# THE SCHOOL FOR INVISIBLE BOYS

## SHAUN DAVID HUTCHINSON

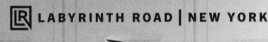 LABYRINTH ROAD | NEW YORK

Text copyright © 2024 by Shaun David Hutchinson
Jacket art copyright © 2024 by Julian Callos

Visit us on the Web! rhcbooks.com

Educators and librarians, for a variety of teaching tools, visit us at RHTeachersLibrarians.com

*Library of Congress Cataloging-in-Publication Data*
Names: Hutchinson, Shaun David, author.
Title: School for invisible boys / Shaun David Hutchinson.
Description: First edition. | New York: Labyrinth Road, 2024. |
Series: The Kairos Files; 1 | Audience: Ages 8–12. | Audience: Grades 4–6. |
Summary: When the normally unseen sixth grader Hector discovers he can turn invisible, he learns that he is not the only invisible boy at his school and there are worse things than bullies lurking the halls.
Identifiers: LCCN 2023031455 (print) | LCCN 2023031456 (ebook) |
ISBN 978-0-593-64629-8 (hardcover) | ISBN 978-0-593-64630-4 (library binding) |
ISBN 978-0-593-64631-1 (ebook)
Subjects: CYAC: Invisibility—Fiction. | Bullies and bullying—Fiction. |
Private schools—Fiction. | Schools—Fiction. | Monsters—Fiction. | Fantasy. |
LCGFT: Fantasy fiction. | Novels.
Classification: LCC PZ7.H96183 Sc 2024 (print) | LCC PZ7.H96183 (ebook) |
DDC [Fic]—dc23

The text of this book is set in 12.5-point Adobe Jenson Pro.

Editor: Liesa Abrams
Cover Designer: Carol Ly
Interior Designer: Jen Valero
Copy Editor: Barbara Bakowski
Managing Editor: Rebecca Vitkus
Production Manager: Natalia Dextre

Printed in the United States of America
10 9 8 7 6 5 4 3 2 1
First Edition

Random House Children's Books supports the First Amendment and celebrates the right to read.

FOR ALL THE LIBRARIANS AND TEACHERS
WHO MADE *THIS* INVISIBLE BOY FEEL SEEN

# 1

**I LOVED TO RUN.** I never felt so free as when I was racing the wind with the sun on my face and no particular place to go.

Running from my ex–best friend because he was dead set on trying to tie my legs into a square knot didn't fill me with the same exhilaration.

"You're roadkill when I catch you, Hector!"

I thought of at least three devastating comebacks to shout over my shoulder, but I needed to save my breath to stay ahead of Blake Nesbitt. He loved to run too, and for as long as I'd known him, he'd been a little faster than me.

It had started in the locker room. I'd just finished changing out of my school uniform into my gym clothes when Blake attacked me for no reason. I was so surprised that I stumbled to the side, which was the only reason I managed to avoid his punch. I couldn't believe that Blake was actually trying to hit me! I'd never seen him hit *any-one* before. I turned to the other boys for help, but they looked away like they were too scared to get between me and Blake. With no help coming, I made a break for the door.

The moment I hit open air, I put on a burst of speed and sprinted toward the PE field, looking for somewhere to hide. I couldn't let Blake catch me or I was a goner for sure. I could run for the bleachers, which wouldn't offer much protection, or try for the trees at the edge of the field, but if Coach caught me there, Blake would be the least of my problems.

There was one other place I could hide. Behind the field stood the old clergy house, a two-story building with filthy windows that screamed, *I am definitely haunted!* It was the last original building from the 1950s, when St. Lawrence's Catholic School for Boys had been built. There were rumors of a ghost that lurked around the old clergy house, and I was a believer, as were most of the boys at St. Lawrence's. Under normal circumstances, I wouldn't have gone within ten yards of that place, but I hoped Blake's fear of the ghost would keep him from following me. When I reached the building, I skidded to a stop to catch my breath.

*"Hector! Over here!"*

And then I stopped breathing. The hot, humid air grew chilly. The skin on my arms turned to chicken flesh, and the hair on the back of my neck rose. I looked around to make sure it wasn't another boy playing a prank on me, but

I was alone behind the clergy house, as far as I could tell, and I didn't recognize the voice. It grated across my ears and felt like an itch in my brain.

*"Hurry up, Hector!"*

I was imagining things. That had to be it. Because the alternative was that the ghost at St. Lawrence's was talking to me and knew my name.

A shout from the field broke me from my stupor. Blake was getting closer. I didn't know what to do. Follow a ghost I couldn't see or take my chances with Blake? I had no idea what the ghost wanted with me, but Blake's intentions were pretty clear.

*"This way, Hector!"*

I chose the ghost.

Quickly but quietly, I crept around to the rear of the building, sticking close to the wall. When St. Lawrence's was founded, the clergy house was where the priests lived. Now the school used it to store desks, textbooks, sports equipment, and whatever junk they didn't need at the main building. Not that I'd ever been inside. It was strictly off-limits to students. Derrick Boyd swore he'd snuck in once and that he'd seen spiders as big as footballs scurrying around and slimy black mold growing on the walls. Derrick also claimed his sister was an android, his parents were international art thieves, and that he'd caught a great white shark while fishing at the beach, so I doubted he'd ever actually been in the clergy house.

It didn't look like I was getting in either. Both the knob

and the dead bolt above it were locked, and no matter how hard I shook the door, it didn't budge. "If someone's there, please let me in!" Shutters covered the first-floor windows, probably to keep out kids like me.

I was toast. The kind that's so burnt you can't save it no matter how much peanut butter you cover it with. A wave of hopelessness washed over me. It was like someone had scooped out the happiness inside me and left me empty. I wanted to quit. Blake was going to win anyway. In fifth grade, I'd been taller than Blake, but he'd sprouted a few inches over the summer, leaving me the runt of the sixth-grade litter. He was bigger and stronger and faster than me. I should give up now.

There was a click, and when I looked, the dead bolt was unlocked.

"What the . . ." I reached for the knob again.

"You're dead, Hector!" Blake Nesbitt burst into view around the corner. I didn't think; I just ran. But this time I wasn't fast enough. I made it as far as the field before Blake caught up to me. He tackled me from behind. We hit the grass, and I barely had time to flip onto my back before he was straddling me, pummeling my stomach and ribs. I was so shocked that he was actually hitting me that it took me a second before I remembered to defend myself.

"I know it was you, Hector!" Blake spit the words, his rage accelerating them to the speed of bullets.

I struggled to get free, but I was better at running than fighting, and look how well that had gone. "I didn't do anything!" There was no way I could escape, so I did my best to protect my face.

"You burned my science project!" Blake shouted. "Musser gave me a zero 'cause I had nothing to turn in!"

The boys from the east and west sixth-grade classes gathered around to watch Blake clobber me. A few even cheered him on. I kept hoping Alex or Gordi or Evan would break up the fight, but they never came.

Blake dug his knee into my thigh. "Admit it! Admit you set my science project on fire!"

Blake Nesbitt only lived a few blocks from me, so it had been easy to bike to his house, hop the fence into his backyard, where he'd spray-painted his project and left it to dry, and light the diorama on fire. I'd felt a sense of justice watching the dinosaurs melt into puddles of plastic at the base of Blake's papier-mâché volcano. And even though I'd had a good reason for destroying Blake's project, a teeny-tiny part of me felt guilty Colonel Musser had flunked him.

"Your project was probably so bad that it lit itself on fire!" Okay, not *that* guilty.

As Blake pulled back to take another swing, a meaty hand grabbed his wrist and lifted him off me. I scurried backward, sore but unbroken.

Coach Barbary loomed over me and Blake, looking down on us like Zeus from Olympus, prepared to smite us with a bolt of lightning. "You boys have exactly three seconds to explain what's going on, or you'll wish you'd never been born."

Yeah, it was way too late for that.

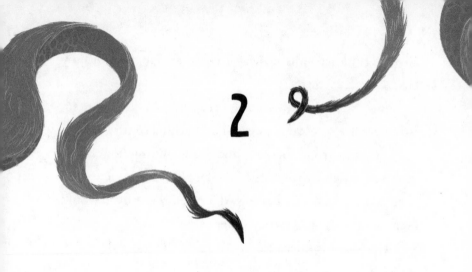

# 2

COACH ULYSSES EUGENE BARBARY had probably started shaving in the first grade. Every day, he wore a polyester polo shirt tucked into polyester shorts at least one size too small; knee-high white socks and sneakers, and a whistle on a cord around his neck. A bristly jungle of fur spilled from the V of his shirt and crawled up his neck, where it mingled with his bushy beard, and his muscled arms were thicker than my chest. I suspected there was a bear hiding in the branches of Coach Barbary's family tree.

"I asked you boys a question, and I expect an answer. Promptly." Coach Barbary's voice was a raspy low growl.

I stole a glance at Blake. He had his eyes aimed at the ground and his lips pressed tightly together. Even though Blake had started the fight, I didn't think it was a good idea to tell Coach. This was between me and Blake, and I still hoped I could get through to him.

Coach Barbary shifted the full power of his glare to me. "On your feet, Griggs."

Breathing hurt, and I winced as I stood.

"Suck it up," Coach Barbary said. "I've got a two-year-old nephew who can throw a harder punch than Nesbitt."

The other boys snickered.

Coach Barbary towered over me and Blake, giving off angry-dad-on-a-road-trip vibes. "Fine. If you boys won't talk, then you can run—"

Blake finally broke his silence. "That's not fair!"

"And if neither of you tells me who started this fight, then you can keep running every day until one of you talks." Coach crossed his arms over his chest. "Go on. Get moving."

Despite the pain, I took off after Blake, jogging laps around the PE field, broiling under the scorching Florida sun. Every agonizing step was a reminder that Coach was essentially punishing me for being used as a punching bag. But there was no arguing with him. If Coach Barbary had any humanity, he kept it deep down in his fungus-infected little piggies.

Blake's longer legs gave him a slight advantage, and I expected him to leave me behind. Instead he fell in beside me. He was radiating hatred, broadcasting it like a radio tower, and I had no way to tune it out.

Like I said, Blake used to be my best friend.

I was in the middle of fourth grade when my mom got remarried. My stepdad had two sons—two and three years older than me—who went to St. Lawrence's, and my mom decided that even though I wasn't Catholic, it would be convenient if we attended the same school. So she pulled me away from my familiar world and dropped me onto this alien planet with no girls where I was expected to attend mass and wear an ugly uniform. Being the new kid was bad enough, but most of the boys at St. Lawrence's already knew each other and weren't interested in getting to know me.

Blake was the exception. We both liked comic books, and we were obsessed with JRPGs like *Dragon Quest* and *Final Fantasy*. He introduced me to some of his friends and offered to show me the ropes and keep me out of trouble. It turned out he was usually the one who got us *into* trouble, but I didn't mind. We spent the rest of the school year and all summer together. Blake was my first real best friend. I'd never met anyone I felt I could talk to about anything, even embarrassing stuff. But Blake always listened, and he never laughed. We became inseparable. I thought we were going to be friends forever.

Until two weeks ago.

"You started this," I said.

Blake snorted.

"If you leave me alone, I'll leave you alone. Okay?"

Blake's sneer was venomous. He acted and sounded nothing like my best friend. "No deal. By the time I'm through with you, Hector, you're gonna regret ever lighting that match." He shot forward, lengthening the distance between us.

"I used a lighter," I said, but Blake was already too far gone.

# 3

I SAT IN the back of my stepdad's cop car thinking about how everything had gone so wrong. My stepbrother Jason was beside me, telling a story that involved pizza sauce shooting out of someone's nose, and he was laughing so hard he was snorting. Jason was in eighth grade, and he looked like his dad—round-cheeked and freckled—though he still had all of his hair. The sound of his voice made me wish I didn't have ears. But I tried to ignore him so I could think about what had happened at the clergy house. The dead bolt had been locked, and then it wasn't. The ghost had to have unlocked it, but I couldn't come up with a good reason why it had tried to help me.

"Hector got into a fight during PE."

Hearing my name dragged me from my thoughts. I rounded on Jason, anger flaring. "Shut up!"

Pop looked at me in the rearview mirror as he drove.

Only half his attention was on the road, and he was constantly drifting into other lanes. "Did you win?"

It had felt weird calling my stepdad by his name, but I hadn't been comfortable calling him Dad, either. My dad lived in Texas. I only got to stay with him for part of the summer and some holidays, but I didn't want him to think I was replacing him, so I'd settled on calling my stepdad Pop.

Before I could answer Pop's question, Jason said, "Heard he cried to Coach Barbary." He rubbed his eyes and fake sobbed.

"Is that true?" Pop asked.

"No," I said.

Pop glanced back at me again. "No, you weren't in a fight, or no, you didn't cry to your coach?"

"It wasn't a fight," I said. "Blake and I just had an argument."

Jason punched me in the arm. He and Pop called it "playing," but playing with my other friends rarely left me with so many bruises. "Heard Coach made them run laps."

One of the disadvantages of attending a small school with my stepbrother was that it was impossible to keep secrets. If there were advantages, I hadn't discovered them.

"I thought you and Blake were friends," Pop said.

I hung my head and mumbled, "Not anymore."

"You've got to learn to stand up for yourself, Hector," Pop said.

Jason snickered. "He'd be better off learning to run faster."

I hugged my backpack to my chest and didn't speak

again until Pop missed the turn to my piano teacher's house. "Where are you going? I've got a lesson today, remember?"

"We need to pick up new cleats for Jason before baseball practice."

It felt like the air in the car had gotten thinner. "I can't miss my lesson."

"Don't get worked up about it. Your mom will call your teacher to explain."

Jason elbowed me in the side. "You're such a pianist." He left the *T* mostly silent and laughed.

"But—"

"It's done. Enough whining about it." Pop had made up his mind that Jason's baseball practice was more important than my piano lesson, and I couldn't change it.

"Whatever," I mumbled barely loud enough for Jason to hear. "At least I get to play at *my* practices."

Jason waited until Pop was distracted to hit me as hard as he could in the thigh. I bit my lip and blinked back tears. "Dead leg," he whispered. Louder, he added, "Geez, Dad, maybe we should take Hector to his stupid lesson. He's so upset about it that he's crying."

Pop shook his head. "Suck it up, Hector. Boys in this family don't cry."

But I wanted to cry. I wanted to scream at them to listen to me. To leave me alone. To stop treating me like *I* was the problem. I didn't, though, because that would have only made it worse. Instead I wiped my tears, kept my eyes forward so I could ignore Jason gloating, and said, "Yes, sir."

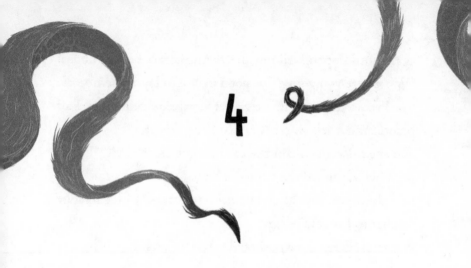

**4**

**ALL I DID** was ask Blake if he wanted to be my boyfriend.

We were walking across the parking lot from the cafeteria to the main building after lunch. Me, Blake, and the rest of the guys we hung out with. Alex Lee was trying to organize a sleepover for his birthday, even though it was still months away, and Greg McAllister was telling a story no one was listening to. I hung back with Blake until I was sure none of the other boys were listening, and asked.

I'd been thinking about it for a while. It made sense. We were already best friends. Of all the people I knew, Blake was the one I wanted to hang out with most. Being boyfriends just felt right to me. I knew most boys wanted girlfriends, but I never had, and I didn't see why it should be a big deal. Besides, Blake had two moms, so I didn't figure he'd think it was weird either. I assumed the worst thing that would happen was that he'd say no.

Blake stopped walking and stared at me. His lip curled and his eyebrows knitted together. He was looking at me like I was a monster. Blake had never looked at me like that before, and it felt worse than the time I'd eaten bad shrimp and spent two days puking.

Then he called me a freak, except *freak* wasn't the word he used. Even my stepbrothers didn't use the word Blake called me. He said it a second time and told me to stay away from him. That we weren't friends anymore.

The next day, Blake still refused to talk to me, and my other friends were ignoring me too. I begged Blake to tell me why he was so mad, but he kept calling me that name and refused to answer my questions.

At first I was just lonely, but then I got angry. I hadn't done anything wrong, and Blake had turned on me, said awful things, and convinced our friends to act like I didn't exist. That was when I decided to set his science project on fire.

I knew it was wrong, but the whole time I was watching it burn, I kept thinking that if Blake didn't want to be my boyfriend, all he'd had to say was "No thank you."

Of course, instead of making me feel better, destroying Blake's project had made everything so much worse.

- - - - - -

Mom's singing drifted into the dining room where I was finishing my homework. Pop was with Jason at baseball practice, and Lee was locked in his room, so it was quiet for once. I had so much on my mind that I could barely concentrate on my worksheet. All I could think about was Blake and the ghost and that the ghost knew my name!

Lots of kids at school had a story about the ghost—objects disappearing, feeling like someone was watching them when they were alone, doors slamming shut—but as far as I knew, the ghost hadn't spoken to anyone else. The first time I'd heard about the ghost, I was in the room I shared with Jason, playing *Mario Kart* with Blake back when we were still friends. His moms had let him spend the night, and it was late.

"You'll never catch me now!" Blake sped away as Princess Peach tossed a bomb that sent my car spinning.

Lee barged into the room without knocking. "What're you doing screaming like a couple of girls?"

"You know who else screams like a girl?" Blake said without looking away from the game. "Valkyries, right before they kick your butt."

Lee muttered something under his breath that I was glad I couldn't hear. I hoped he'd leave. Instead he came all the way in and sat on the edge of my bed. "You hear about the ghost at school yet?"

I was already so far behind in the game that I didn't stand a chance of winning, so I looked over my shoulder and said, "What ghost?"

"You haven't told him?" Lee asked Blake.

Blake crossed the finish line and dropped his controller. "There's a ghost at school." He looked at me, then Lee, before rolling his eyes.

"You better be careful," Lee said.

"Why?"

Lee looked around like he was telling us a secret. "You know that eighth grader with the patch of white hair?"

I nodded. I didn't know his name, but I'd heard people call him a skunk. I thought the white streak in his hair looked cool.

"He didn't have that white hair until he saw the ghost while he was using the toilet."

"That's not true!" Blake said. "You're lying."

Lee held up his hands and stood. "Whatever. I just wouldn't use the bathroom alone if I were you." He left the room, shutting the door behind him.

I didn't like the idea of going to a haunted school. "Is it true? Is there really a ghost at St. Lawrence's?"

Blake rested his hand on my shoulder. "Even if there is, you don't have to worry. I've got your back." Then he smiled, and I believed him.

But now the ghost knew my name, and Blake was trying to punch me instead of protect me. Everything was so messed up, and I didn't know how to fix it.

"Want to lick the spoon?" Mom stood at the table holding a wooden spoon coated with creamy chocolate. "I'm making chocolate pudding pie." Under normal circumstances, I would've grabbed the spoon before Lee appeared and stole it—he had a better sense of smell than a bloodhound—but I wasn't in the mood.

"No thank you."

Mom pulled out a chair and sat down at the table. "I know you're upset about missing your lesson, but Jason needed new cleats, and I couldn't get away from work or I would have taken you myself."

"Sure," I said. "Whatever."

Mom frowned. "Being part of a family means sometimes making sacrifices for each other."

"But why is it always me who has to make the sacrifices? We can't have a dog because Lee's allergic, I can't have a lemon meringue pie on my birthday because Jason hates lemons, and instead of going to the library or museums, we have to go to football games or on fishing trips because those are the things Pop and the boys like to do. They even get their favorite toppings when we order pizza. Why can't we just have mushrooms and black olives for once like I want?"

I spit the whole thing out without barely taking a breath. When I finished, my mom said, "Feel better?"

"No."

Mom stuck the spoon in my hand and waited for me to take a grudging lick before she spoke again. "I understand this is tough for you, Hector, but I need you to cut them a little slack."

"Why do you always take their side?"

"There are no sides in a family," Mom said. "Your pop is a good man. I know he doesn't always get you, but he tries."

I spluttered, nearly choking on chocolate.

"He does," Mom said. "In his way. And the boys are . . ." She paused. "Well, they're boys."

"So am I," I mumbled.

"But you see the world differently than they do. They're a little rougher around the edges. I only ask more of you because I know you're capable of it."

I didn't know what to say, so I licked the spoon in silence. I liked being part of the family, most of the time, but I wished Pop and the boys could try to see me for who I was. Sometimes I felt like they didn't see me at all.

"Is there something else going on?" Mom asked. "Roy mentioned you were fighting with Blake?"

I stuck the whole spoon in my mouth and hung my head.

"Is it serious? Should I call Melanie?"

Melanie was Mrs. Nesbitt, one of Blake's moms. I thought about telling my mom the truth, but if I told her what Blake had said and how he'd started the fight, I'd also have to admit I'd set Blake's project on fire. My mom would definitely call Blake's moms then—probably Colonel Musser, too—and we'd both wind up in big trouble. I still hoped I could fix my friendship with Blake, but I'd ruin any chance of that if I got our parents involved.

"Whatever it is, you can tell me," Mom said. "You know I'll love you no matter what."

"I know." The chocolate tasted like sludge, but licking

the spoon gave me something to do instead of spilling my guts about my problems.

Mom sighed and stood. "Well, I'm sure whatever is going on between you boys will work itself out."

"What if it doesn't?" I asked. "What do I do then?"

Mom tousled my hair and took the mostly clean spoon back from me. "It never hurts to say you're sorry. Why don't you start there?"

Maybe Mom was onto something. Maybe if I apologized for asking Blake to be my boyfriend and setting fire to his project, we could go back to the way things were before. I just hoped she was right about it not hurting. I didn't think I could handle any more bruises.

# 5

POP USUALLY DROPPED me and Jason off at school early on his way to work. As soon as we got there, Jason ran off to join his friends playing basketball, and I made my way to the library. It seemed so small, neglected and sandwiched as it was between the school's main building and the massive church, but it was my favorite place at St. Lawrence's Catholic School for Boys.

"Hector Griggs."

I dropped my backpack off on the nearest table. "Hey, Mr. Morhill."

Mr. Morhill looked like a scarecrow in a fancy plaid suit and round wire glasses, but his head wasn't full of straw. He was one of the smartest people I'd ever met. He'd shown up last year to replace Miss Calloway, who'd won the lottery and immediately retired to travel the world. Unlike Miss Calloway, Mr. Morhill allowed students into the library before school. When I didn't have any homework to finish, Mr. Morhill let me practice piano in the music room at the back of the library.

But that morning I wanted—no, I needed—to talk about the haunted clergy house and the ghost. The other teachers and priests at St. Lawrence's thought it was nonsense, but Mr. Morhill was different. He was always asking us boys for stories about the ghost, and he talked about how the world was filled with weird and wonderful things that defied explanation. Mr. Morhill was definitely the strangest librarian I'd ever met, which was one of the reasons I liked him.

As I pulled out a chair to sit, I casually said, "I heard the ghost yesterday."

Mr. Morhill was standing behind the checkout desk, scanning a stack of books into the computer, but as soon as I spoke, he looked at me over the rims of his glasses. "Was that before or after your scuffle with Mr. Nesbitt?"

My cheeks burned. Mr. Morhill had an uncanny knowledge of what was going on around St. Lawrence's. None of the other teachers seemed to care, but Mr. Morhill knew which students were fighting, who was being bullied, who was having trouble at home. If I hadn't known better, I would've sworn he could read our minds. "It was nothing," I mumbled.

"Was that why Gene ordered you to run laps?" Mr. Morhill said. Gene was Coach Barbary. It sounded odd when teachers called each other by their first names.

I'd already decided to take my mom's advice and apologize to Blake, so I wasn't in the mood to discuss it with Mr. Morhill. "Didn't you hear me? The ghost talked to me. It knew my name!"

Mr. Morhill wandered out from behind the desk and sat across from me, folding his hands on the table and giving me his full attention. "I'm listening. Start from the beginning."

"Okay, so I was running—"

"From Mr. Nesbitt?"

I lowered my eyes. "Yeah. Anyway, I didn't know where to go, and this voice called my name. It didn't sound like a student. It was kind of raspy and thin, like Mrs. Ford the time she got bronchitis." I told Mr. Morhill everything. About running toward the old clergy house, about the dead bolt. He listened without interrupting until I was done.

"You didn't go *into* the clergy house, did you?"

I shook my head.

"Is there anything else you remember?" Mr. Morhill asked. "Was it chilly, did you feel the moment of your imminent demise, did you smell anything like sulfur or potato salad that's turned?"

"I didn't smell anything weird. But there was this feeling."

"Yes?" Mr. Morhill said.

"I swear it was coming from the clergy house. It was like someone stole the sun and took all the warmth with it."

Mr. Morhill leaned forward on his elbows. "It *was* cold, then?"

"Yeah," I said. "But the cold was inside me. I don't know how to explain it."

"I think you've done an admirable job." Mr. Morhill bridged his hands and held them to his chin, his eyes distant. "Promise me you won't go near the clergy house again, Hector."

Returning had been the last thing on my mind until Mr. Morhill mentioned it. But now I was curious. "Why? I think the ghost was trying to help me."

"Have you heard of the yellow pitcher plant?"

My mom had a pretty big garden in the backyard at home, but I'd never heard her mention a pitcher plant.

"Found in the south, the *Sarracenia flava* uses its vibrant color and sweet nectar to lure insects into a hollow pitcher, where it traps them and slowly dissolves them in its digestive juices."

"Cool!" Nature was gross, but also awesome.

Mr. Morhill shook his head slowly. "Yes. However, my point is that occasionally, things that appear helpful are, in reality, trying to eat you."

Before I could respond, the library door swung open and Gordi Standish stuck his red head in.

Mr. Morhill looked over his shoulder. "The air-conditioning in this building barely functions as it is, without you letting what little cold air it produces escape, Mr. Standish."

Gordi zeroed in on me. "I was looking for Hector."

"Congratulations," he said. "You've found him."

"Blake asked me to tell you to come outside," Gordi said to me, ignoring Mr. Morhill.

Gordi was one of the guys I used to sit with at lunch. He didn't talk much, and I wasn't sure if it was because he was shy or because he didn't have anything to say. I was surprised Blake had sent Gordi instead of Luke or Arjun. I'd always gotten along with Arjun because he wasn't Catholic either. He was only at St. Lawrence's because his mom taught first grade here. When the other students went for confession, Arjun and I sat in the back pews, each trying to make the other laugh first. Sending Gordi was a strange choice, and it made me wary.

"What for?" I asked.

Gordi shrugged. "He wants to apologize or something."

If there was even a small chance I could patch up my friendship with Blake, I had to take it.

"We'll finish our chat later, Mr. Griggs." Mr. Morhill glanced again at Gordi. "Remember what I said about the pitcher plant."

I followed Gordi out of the library and around the back of the church to a small garden that was off-limits to students. Blake stood under the shade of a gumbo-limbo tree, his lips pinched and his arms crossed over his chest. He was flanked by Evan Christopher and Conrad Eldridge. Evan was the kind of boy who agreed with whoever spoke the loudest, and he was up for anything as long as everyone else was doing it. We'd usually gotten along, but that was before Blake had decided I was the enemy.

Conrad Eldridge was an eighth-grade boy who had a reputation for being a teacher's pet. They loved him because he got straight As and did his homework and always knew the answers to questions when they called on him. He had buzzed brown hair and thick eyebrows. He was also the tallest boy in our school, and his voice was deeper than even Coach Barbary's. I was surprised to find him with Blake.

I stood with my hands in my pockets and my eyes on the ground. With Gordi, Evan, and Conrad attending him, I doubted Blake actually intended to apologize, but I held tightly to hope, refusing to let go. "I'm here."

Conrad whispered into Blake's ear. Blake snickered. "Yeah, I didn't think he'd be stupid enough to come either."

I flinched. Blake was using a lot of words I'd never heard him say before. It might have been pointless, but I decided to carry on with my plan, since I might not get another chance. "I'm sorry, Blake."

Blake had rarely worn anything but a cheerful smile. Even when his moms punished him, he accepted it without complaint. But as he stood under the gumbo-limbo tree, his lips were twisted into a vicious sneer. "Shut up."

"I'm sorry I set your science project on fire."

"Shut up, Hector!"

"And I'm sorry I asked you to be my boyfriend."

Blake lunged forward and shoved me into Gordi. "I told you to shut up!"

The attack caught me off guard. "Stop! This isn't you, Blake!" Tears welled in my eyes.

Conrad whispered to Blake again, and both boys laughed.

"I told you guys he was a *freak*," Blake said, but *freak* wasn't the name he called me. "Hold him."

Gordi pulled my arms behind my back, but he wasn't holding them tightly. "I don't think this is okay."

"Did he really want to be your boyfriend?" Evan Christopher said like it was the funniest joke he'd ever heard. I definitely wasn't laughing.

"What's wrong with you, Blake?" I said. "Why are you doing this?"

"Because you're a *freak*," he said. "And this is what happens to *freaks* at this school."

My mom had been wrong. *Sorry* wasn't going to fix our friendship this time. The Blake calling me names wasn't the best friend I'd spent the summer with, biking around town and eating candy until I was sick. I didn't know the Blake standing in front of me, and I didn't want to.

"You're going to regret we ever met," Blake promised.

I couldn't reason with Blake, and I'd proven the day before that I couldn't fight him. That left me, again, with one option to save myself. I stomped on Gordi's foot as hard as I could, driving the heel of my loafer into his toes. He hollered and loosened his grip on my arms, and I took advantage of the opening to twist free. Gordi reached for me but only managed to grab my backpack. I slipped my arms through the straps and left him holding it while I took off at a dead run.

I was faced with the same dilemma as the day before. Blake was faster and there weren't many places to hide. The main building wasn't open yet, and I doubted I could make it back to the library before Blake, Gordi, Evan, and Conrad caught me. I could've tried to reach Jason, but then he would've told Pop, and I didn't want to hear how I was a crybaby who needed to be tougher. I even considered trying to reach the clergy house—maybe the ghost would help me again—but it was too far away. The church was the only building I had any chance of beating Blake to. Students weren't allowed inside during school hours without permission, but I was prepared to risk detention to prevent another beating from my ex–best friend.

Fueled by fear, I sprinted for St. Lawrence's church. I didn't look back and I didn't slow down until I hit the doors, pulled them open, and stole inside. Churches had been used as sanctuaries throughout history, so I hoped God wouldn't be too upset with me for hiding out even though I wasn't Catholic. I expected Father Allison or Father Carmichael to be there, but the church was empty. Blake and the others couldn't be far behind. I needed to quickly find a nook where I could hide. Luckily, I knew just the place.

There was a small stairway, cleverly concealed behind wood paneling, that led to a balcony where the pipe organ was located. Father Allison had shown it to me once after I'd asked if it was the same as a piano. It wasn't. I was pretty sure Blake wouldn't find me up there. When I reached the balcony, I peeked over the ledge as Blake, Gordi, Evan, and Conrad burst into the church. They weren't even trying to be quiet.

"Find him!" Blake said.

Evan split off, checking the pews, while Gordi crept toward the dais at the front of the church.

"You better come out, Hector!" Blake's voice ricocheted off the stained-glass windows depicting the stations of the cross. "You're only making things worse for yourself."

Blake had every right to be angry at me for setting fire to his project, but I didn't understand why he was so mad at me for asking him to be my boyfriend. He'd told me how kids at school used to pick on him for having two moms and how he hadn't understood why it had bothered them so much, so there had to be something more going on, and if I could figure out what it was, maybe I could fix what I'd broken. But I couldn't do anything if he wouldn't talk to me without calling me bad names.

My legs were trembling as I watched Blake and Conrad snake up and down the pews. They stopped, and Conrad leaned over to whisper to Blake. Blake turned around and looked straight at my hiding spot. I dropped down, praying he hadn't spotted me, or my perfect hiding place would become a dead end. I tucked myself as far back as I could between the organ and the wall and hugged my knees to my chest.

*Don't see me, don't see me, don't see me.*

Blake might not have found the door to the balcony on his own, but Gordi was an altar boy and probably knew where it was. I winced as the hinges squeaked.

*Don't see me, don't see me, don't see me.*

The stairs creaked.

*Don't see me, don't see me. Please don't see me.*

Blake's long shadow crept onto the balcony before him.

I made myself as small as possible, so small that maybe Blake wouldn't notice me. *Don't see me, don't see me.*

The balcony was cramped, barely large enough for two people. Blake scanned the area. He looked right at where I was hiding. I held my breath, waiting for Blake to yank me to my feet by the front of my uniform shirt.

"He up there?" Gordi called from below.

Blake turned away and leaned over the ledge. "I swear I saw him."

"He probably ran out the back." I recognized Evan's voice.

"Yeah," Blake said. "Maybe." He looked around again, his brow furrowed in confusion. Finally he shook his head and left.

I couldn't believe my luck. There was no way Blake hadn't seen me. Maybe he'd pretended not to because he didn't actually want to beat me up and had only said he did because he was trying to impress Conrad. That was probably too much to hope for, but I couldn't think of another reason that made sense.

I counted to one hundred before crawling out of my

hiding place. My knees were shaking as I descended the stairs. I shut the door to the balcony behind me and turned around, nearly running into Father Allison.

"Sorry!" I blurted without thinking.

Father Allison stumbled backward, startled. His eyes were wide behind his thick, round glasses. "Who's there? This is a church, not a playground." He opened the door to look in the staircase, and I had to hop to the side to get out of his way. "Hello?"

"I said 'sorry.'" I waved my hand in front of Father Allison's face. He didn't flinch or move or react at all. He was looking at me the same way Blake had. He was looking *through* me, staring at the door to the pipe organ in confusion.

Something wasn't right. Father Allison wasn't known for his sense of humor, and if this was a joke, I definitely wasn't laughing. Either way, I had to leave before I got in trouble. When I reached the door, I turned and spotted my reflection in the glass door of a notice board on the wall. Or rather, my lack of a reflection. I wouldn't have believed it if I hadn't seen it—or *not* seen it—for myself. I couldn't see my reflection. I held my hand in front of my face. I could see it with my eyes, but when I looked in the glass, I only saw the reflection of the wall behind me. My brain felt like a frozen computer, fans kicking on high as it overheated, trying to process what was happening. All I could do was stare at my hand and the glass, eyes darting back and forth from one to the other.

Blake hadn't seen me. Father Allison hadn't seen me either. Maybe Blake was pretending, but Father Allison would have definitely told me off if he knew I was in here. Then there was the glass. I'd never heard of trick glass that didn't reflect people, and even if it existed, why would they have it in the church? There was only one explanation.

I was invisible!

# 6

I LEFT THE church and returned to the garden to retrieve my backpack. I was having a difficult time believing I was actually invisible. The problem was that no other answer I came up with accounted for why Blake and Father Allison hadn't been able to see me or why I didn't have a reflection. And if I was invisible, how had it happened? Was I a superhero now? Was I going to be stuck like this forever?

I found my backpack in the garden. My books and notebook and papers had been dumped and scattered on the grass. When I leaned over to grab my math homework, my hand passed through it. I reached for my social studies book, but it was like trying to touch smoke. This couldn't be happening. I rested my palm against the trunk of a gumbo-limbo tree and was reassured to feel solid bark under my hand, yet I couldn't pick up my backpack.

A shrill bell sounded in the distance, announcing it was

time to assemble into homeroom groups. That bell meant I had five minutes before our teachers would lead us inside. My stomach hurt, and I thought I was going to be sick. I'd get in so much trouble if I wasn't in class. I needed to turn visible again, but I didn't know how. And what was I going to do about my backpack?

Finally I decided to leave my bag for later and raced to where the 6W class had gathered. Each grade was divided into east and west groups. Mr. Grady taught English to the sixth, seventh, and eighth graders, and was also the 6W homeroom teacher. I waited for someone to notice me, but no one did. They didn't see me; they didn't hear me. To them, I didn't exist.

Blake stood with Evan Christopher in the 6E line, his arms crossed over his chest. He looked as if the only thing that would make him happy was ripping the legs off grasshoppers.

Mr. Grady clapped his hands and called for his students to follow him inside. Since no one could see me, I had to step quickly to avoid being jostled. When we got upstairs, I ducked into the restroom and stood in front of the mirror, marveling again at my invisibility. There wasn't so much as a shimmer to give me away. But, as amazing as it was, I had less than five minutes before Mr. Grady would notice I wasn't in my seat. If that happened, he'd mark me absent, which would trigger a call to Mom or Pop, and then I'd really be in trouble.

"Come on," I begged. "Turn visible!" I squeezed my eyes shut and held my breath and tensed every muscle in my body, but when I opened my eyes, nothing had changed.

I really was going to be stuck like this for the rest of my life. No one would see me. My parents would think I'd run away, and eventually they'd forget me. Hot tears welled in my eyes. I could practically hear Lee telling me not to be a baby, Jason making "boo-hoo" sounds, and Pop telling me boys didn't cry. But if there was ever a time for tears, this was it. I almost wouldn't have minded the name-calling if it meant they could see me.

The warning bell rang. Ninety seconds until I was officially late for class.

Getting upset wasn't going to help, so I took a deep breath and tried to relax. Using a trick my piano teacher had taught me when I'd had trouble playing a piece of music, I clenched my muscles, starting at my toes and working my way up, and then slowly released them.

*Please turn visible. Please.*

A flicker. So quick I nearly missed it.

I breathed in slowly and exhaled. *Please turn visible.*

Steadily, my image in the mirror shimmered and solidified. There I was. My dad's big nose and straight hair, front teeth that poked out, making it hard to close my mouth all the way. That face staring back at me was the most beautiful sight I'd seen in ages. But I didn't have time to admire my reflection. I raced out of the restroom, down the hall, and into homeroom right as the final bell rang. The other students, already seated, turned to stare. Mr. Grady looked up, his mouth set in a grim frown.

"Restroom," I said breathlessly.

Mr. Grady shook his head. "Be quicker about it next time, Hector."

Relieved to have made it at all, I said, "Yes, sir."

# 7

MY BODY MIGHT have been in the classroom, but my mind was stuck in the church. As we moved from homeroom to my other classes, I kept thinking about what had happened, trying to figure out *how* it had happened. Blake had been coming up the stairs to the balcony and I'd wished for him to not be able to see me. Had someone heard and granted my wish? Was it a miracle? An answered prayer? Could it have been the ghost? I didn't know. And worse was that I didn't know where to begin looking for answers. Turning invisible was huge, almost too big to wrap my brain around, so I focused on a problem that was slightly more manageable. What was Blake doing with Conrad Eldridge? Aside from being in eighth grade, Conrad wasn't the type of person Blake would have been friends with before. Conrad had the teachers fooled into thinking he was a good student, but everyone else knew he could be vicious.

There were stories about him picking on first and second graders for fun, and I believed them. If Blake and Conrad were friends now, Blake was further gone than I'd thought.

"Well, Hector?"

Colonel Musser and most of my classmates were staring at me, waiting for me to do something, but I had no idea what. "Um . . ."

"If you can't list the steps of the scientific method," Musser said, "then you can at least tell us what you're day-dreaming about that's so much more interesting than my lesson."

The class laughed. I caught Gordi watching me curiously. He was probably only interested so he could report back to Blake, but I was more worried about Musser.

Colonel Musser wore polyester trousers and a short-sleeve button-down shirt, kept her silver hair buzzed short, drove a Harley motorcycle to school, and looked old enough to have forgotten more about science than I had ever learned. As far as I knew, she'd never served in any branch of the military, but her nickname had been passed from class to class like a note in a bottle for as long as anyone could remember. Colonel Musser was strict, but she was also fair and had a wicked sense of humor. A student who could make her laugh could usually weasel out of all but the worst trouble.

I'd never managed to make her laugh, but, luckily, I'd read ahead and knew the answer. "Ask a question," I said, ticking off the steps on my fingers. "Make a hypothesis, test the hypothesis with an experiment, review the results, compare the results to the hypothesis, and report the findings."

Colonel Musser smiled. It wasn't quite a laugh, but it was close enough. "Excellent. But keep your head in my class and out of the clouds, okay?"

I'd fully intended to do what she said, but talking about the scientific method had given me an idea.

**Question:** How had I turned invisible?

**Hypothesis:** When I'd become invisible, I'd been terrified and focused on nothing but remaining unseen. It had been the same for turning visible. Therefore, turning invisible required intense concentration. And, possibly, a little fear.

**Experiment:** Find a quiet place where I wouldn't be disturbed and attempt to become invisible again.

I had other questions I wanted to answer. Like, since my clothes had also been invisible, would any objects I was holding change with me? What would happen if I became invisible and then kicked off one of my shoes? Would the shoe turn visible? Was I only invisible to people or could dogs see me? What about cameras? Why was I able to touch the doors to the church and the restroom but unable to pick up my backpack? And why hadn't Father Allison heard me when I'd spoken? But my top priority was to test my hypothesis, and I knew exactly when and where to do it.

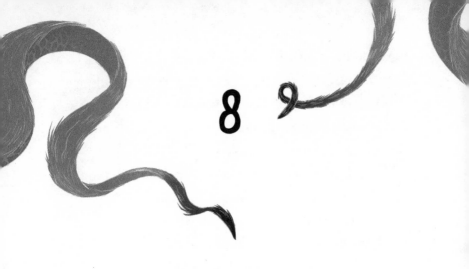

**8**

**LUNCH PERIOD WAS** five hundred boys ages six to thirteen crammed into a small cafeteria that also served as the place where assemblies, graduation ceremonies, and school plays were held, while a rotating group of teachers spent the hour rushing from table to table threatening students with detentions and trips to Principal O'Shea's office. It was loud, it was rowdy. It was the perfect opportunity to sneak away and test my hypothesis.

I walked to the cafeteria with the rest of the 6W class, but the moment we were through the doors, I split off and snuck down the hallway to the restrooms. There were two, and one was out of order so often that the janitor used it as a supply closet. I ducked inside and locked the door behind me. I was tired from running laps for Coach Barbary in PE, but that didn't dampen my excitement.

Blake and I used to sit together at lunch, but since our

fight, I'd been eating with the cupcakes, a table of sixth- and seventh-grade outcasts. I hadn't asked if I could sit with them, and they hadn't said I couldn't. Even if they noticed I was missing, I doubted they would care.

I shifted a mop bucket out of the way so I could stand in front of the sink and watch myself in the mirror. "Don't see me. Don't see me. Don't see me."

I wasn't sure the words were necessary, but I whispered them anyway.

"Don't see me, don't see me, don't see me."

I concentrated on how scared I'd felt in the church. When my mom and I had moved in with Pop, Jason, and Lee, I'd been demoted from the star of the show to a supporting character without any lines. There had been days when I'd felt like Blake was the only person who noticed I existed.

"Don't see me, don't see me, don't see me."

Now I was standing beside a busted toilet wishing for Blake to not see me at all.

My body shimmered, exposing the tile wall behind me. I kept concentrating, thinking about becoming invisible, and I watched in the mirror as I disappeared completely. I held up my hand. I could still see it in front of my face, but it no longer cast a reflection.

I'd done it! I was invisible! I pumped my fist in the air and hooted. My first thought was how excited Blake was going to be when I told him. Then I remembered that Blake was the reason I'd become invisible in the first place, and my excitement dimmed.

"Calm down," I said to myself. It was only a superpower if I could change back.

I took a deep breath and held it as I imagined myself visible again. My lungs burned, and just as panic began to creep in, my body reappeared. It was ghostly at first but solidified rapidly.

I whooped and danced around the cramped room.

**Conclusion:** I could turn invisible at will! I was basically a superhero. The Invisible Boy. No, I needed a better name. Something catchy. The See-Through Super? Gaseous Guy? The Hidden Hero? Blake was usually better at coming up with stuff like that, but he only seemed to want to call me one name in particular these days.

My experiment complete, I turned to leave but stopped before opening the door. I'd proven I could turn invisible, but now I had an opportunity to test the limits of my power, and I shouldn't pass it up. Besides, my lunch was in my backpack, which was still behind the church, so practicing being invisible would give me something to do besides listen to my stomach rumble.

*Don't see me.* Much quicker than before, I faded from sight. I opened the door and slipped into the hallway. At first I crept along, trying not to make noise, but Father Allison hadn't heard me talking directly to him, so I figured no one would hear my footsteps over the roar of five hundred boys shouting, chewing, and making fart noises.

I kept waiting for someone to look my way, to point at me or laugh, or for a teacher to tell me to get back to my seat, but no one did. I wandered up and down the rows of tables unnoticed. As I passed a group of fourth graders, I tried to tap one on the shoulder, but my hand passed through him. I didn't understand why I could open doors and lean against walls but couldn't touch anything else.

I spotted Jason at his regular table with his friends. I never went anywhere near him during school unless I absolutely couldn't help it, and I wondered what they talked about. Baseball, apparently. Jason was bragging about how many runs he'd scored during his last game, but none of it was true. As much as Jason loved baseball, he wasn't very good. He struck out more often than anyone on his team. It didn't surprise me that Jason lied to his friends, but it made me feel bad for him. What did it matter if he wasn't any good? I was terrible at video games, but I still loved to play them.

Bored, I drifted toward Blake's table.

"I swear I saw him on the balcony before I went up," I overheard Blake say when I got closer. "There has to be another way down."

"There isn't," Gordi said. "And why do you hate him so much now anyway?"

"Because he's a *freak*."

Gordi pursed his lips, looking confused. "Don't you have two moms?"

Blake punched Gordi in the shoulder, and not in a playful way. Prior to the day before, I'd never seen Blake hit anyone, not even as a joke. It had been surprising when he'd attacked me in the locker room, but at least then I'd kind of understood his reasons. Seeing him hit Gordi for speaking the truth made me wonder if that was even really Blake or just an alien wearing his skin as a suit.

The other boys, Alex and Greg and Arjun and Evan and Luke, looked surprised too, but none of them spoke up. Conrad was sitting on Blake's other side, which was odd because most eighth-grade boys wouldn't be caught dead at a sixth-grade table. I felt like I'd been transported to a parallel world where Blake was a bully and we'd never been friends.

"What was that for?" Gordi rubbed his shoulder. "I just thought Hector was your best friend. That's all."

Blake tore into his sandwich like it had insulted his grandma. "I only let Hector think we were friends because I felt sorry for him."

Gordi looked away, but the other boys, the boys who'd picked me to be on their kickball teams and invited me to their sleepovers, began calling me the same unspeakable name Blake had. They were laughing. They were laughing at me even though they couldn't see me. Every time I heard one of them say that name, it physically hurt. *Freak* was a kick to the gut. *Freak* was a punch to the nose. *Freak* was a knee to the crotch that knocked the wind out of me and left me wanting to throw up.

I couldn't listen anymore. I ran from the cafeteria, across the parking lot, and into the school building. I sat in the stairwell and shook as hot, invisible tears rolled down my cheeks. They were supposed to be my friends. Blake was supposed to be my *best* friend.

It was the middle of fourth grade. I'd been a new student at St. Lawrence's for two weeks and I hadn't talked to anyone. I missed my old school and my old friends, and fourth grade was so much harder than third grade had been. I stood on the PE field with the other boys in my class while Blake Nesbitt and Nick Price picked teams for soccer. I hung out in the back, kicking the grass with my sneaker.

"I'll take . . . Hector."

I looked up. No one was more surprised to hear Blake say my name than me. Nobody had ever picked me first for anything. I pointed at myself, and Blake nodded and waved for me to join him. When I jogged over, I whispered, "Why'd you choose me? I'm really bad at soccer."

"I saw you reading a book about dragons," Blake said. "I like dragons too."

"How's that going to help us win the game?"

Blake shrugged. "I'd rather lose on a team with people I like than win with people I don't. You should come over to my house after school sometime. You play video games, right?"

Blake and I were a team from that day on. Until I ruined everything.

"Don't cry. Crying attracts *it*."

I looked up and spotted a boy at the top of the stairs staring right at me. He was stocky, with round cheeks and big eyes behind black glasses, and he was wearing a St. Lawrence's uniform. I didn't recognize him, but I figured I would have, since there was only one Black boy at St. Lawrence's that I knew of. I was so surprised, for a second I forgot what had happened in the cafeteria. "You can see me?"

The boy's eyes widened and his mouth fell open. "You can see *me?*"

I stood and wiped my eyes with the back of my hand. "Of course."

Relief flooded the boy's face. He stumbled halfway down the stairs, nearly tripping over his feet. "My name's Orson Wellington. You have to help me." He spoke so quickly that his words rammed into each other like bumper cars. "I'm stuck here. Stuck like this. It's been years. The gelim's hunting me and it'll get you, too—" He looked over his shoulder. "I have to go!"

The boy ran. I called his name and started up the stairs after him, but before I took two steps, Coach Barbary stomped into the stairwell. He looked around, cocking his head like a dog listening for a familiar sound, until his eyes landed on where I was standing. For a second it seemed like he was looking *at* me, but I was still invisible. I held my breath anyway, not daring to make a sound.

Finally, Coach Barbary shook his head and left.

**9**

## WHO IS ORSON WELLINGTON?

That was the question that kept running through my mind. Who was he? What had he been scared of? With five hundred students at St. Lawrence's, it was impossible to know each name, but I still recognized most of their faces. Especially the boys in the upper grades, since I passed them in the hallway between classes multiple times per day. If I'd had any money, I would have bet that I'd never seen Orson Wellington in my life.

I thought about Orson the rest of the day, all night at home, and even in my sleep. I woke up still thinking about Orson, and I was so distracted during my classes that I got yelled at to pay attention by two different teachers. It occurred to me that Orson might be the ghost. His might have been the voice I'd heard at the clergy house two days earlier, though they hadn't sounded alike. But how had I seen him in the stairwell, and how had he seen me? Maybe I was a ghost, too, except that didn't make sense, because ghosts were spirits of the dead, and Blake hadn't managed to kill me yet. Maybe turning invisible had given me the ability to see and hear ghosts. Or maybe Orson wasn't a ghost at all. But if he *was* the ghost, then that meant he was dead, and since he was in a St. Lawrence's uniform, he'd probably died at the school, which wasn't a totally scary thought that would definitely give me nightmares.

When fifth-period PE rolled around, I changed in the locker room and then trudged to the field, where Coach Barbary was waiting for me. He caught my eye and crooked his finger, calling me over. Then he did the same to Blake.

"Are you boys ready to tell me why you were fighting?"

I looked at my feet.

"Then get to running."

I took off at a jog around the PE field and tried to ignore the sounds of the other boys having fun while I was stuck doing laps. Blake jogged beside me, though I wished he wouldn't. I could still hear what he'd said about me at lunch. How he'd only been my friend because he felt sorry for me.

People like to repeat that song about sticks and stones, but words *do* hurt. Sometimes they hurt more because they leave wounds no one can see. In spite of how bruised Blake's words had left me, I *still* wanted to be his friend, and I thought that maybe, without any of the other boys around, I finally had an opportunity to convince him to stop acting so mean. Before our fight, Blake would've been the first person I told about Orson Wellington and turning invisible, so I figured that was a good place to start.

"The ghost is real, by the way."

Blake grunted.

"I heard it Monday by the clergy house. It said my name. And I saw someone yesterday. A kid in a school uniform." I wasn't sure if Orson Wellington and the ghost were the same thing, but it was too much to explain to Blake while we were running.

"In the church?" Blake asked, trying not to sound interested.

"Stairwell in the main building." Sweat kept rolling into my eyes, and all I could do was blink it away. "I think he was a student."

Blake snorted. "Probably someone who died of boredom in Mrs. Ford's class."

A laugh bubbled up out of me. "Croaked mid-snore."

"And now he's trapped at this school forever, stuck listening to Mrs. Ford's lecture about the Oh-ra-gan Trail." Laughter shook Blake's shoulders. For a second he seemed like my best friend again, so I took a chance.

"I'm sorry about your science project. I shouldn't have set it on fire."

Blake's smile evaporated. "Shut up, *freak*."

I flinched. "Come on, Blake. Tell me what I did to make you so angry. This isn't like you." I knew I sounded pathetic, but I didn't care.

"Tell me how you got down from the balcony first," he said.

A month ago, I wouldn't have hesitated. I would have explained about turning invisible, and the look on Father Allison's face when the door leading to the pipe organ seemed to open on its own. But a month ago, I would have been telling my best friend. Now I wasn't sure what we were, and I didn't want to give up my only advantage.

"I don't know what you're talking about."

"Liar," Blake sneered. "I saw you up there."

"Maybe it was your new best friend playing a trick on you."

Blake's hatred for me radiated off him, and that hurt more than sticks and stones and words combined.

"You'll tell me," Blake said. "One way or another."

The last embers of my hope that Blake and I could rescue our friendship grew cold. "If you hate me so much," I said, my voice cracking, "why don't you just leave me alone?"

Blake glanced at me, then toward the school before facing forward again. "Because *he* won't let me."

# 10

I WAS BEING haunted by two ghosts—Orson Wellington and Blake Nesbitt—and I didn't know what to do about either. So when I got home, I retreated to my piano, the one place where things made sense.

When Mom and Pop had gotten married and we'd moved into his house, Pop had claimed there wasn't room for the instrument. The piano meant more to me than anything else I owned, including all my books and toys, and I'd threatened to run away if they got rid of it. Luckily, Mom cleared space in a corner of her office, where I could play and wouldn't disturb anyone but her.

Playing piano allowed me to shut out the world when it became too loud. No matter how bad my day was, music made it a little less awful. And it was one of the few things Blake wasn't good at, but he never put me down for it. Sometimes he even hung out and watched me practice.

"I wish I could play," Blake said after school one day.

I was playing *Solfeggietto* to warm up, but quickly transitioned into the *Legend of Zelda* theme song. "You probably could if you tried."

"Nah. Not like you."

I felt my cheeks turn red. "I'm not even that good."

"Yeah you are," Blake said.

"Well, I wish I was good at baseball or football or something."

Blake grunted. "Half the boys at St. Lawrence's are good at sports, but none of them can do what you can. Besides, it's not like Orpheus convinced Hades to let him bring Eurydice back from the dead by throwing a perfect spiral." Blake had gotten interested in Greek mythology after I told him where my name came from, and my mom had given him some books, which he'd devoured.

"That didn't work out very well for him in the end, though, did it?"

"Maybe not," Blake said, "but it wasn't the music that let him down. It was that he didn't trust himself enough."

Mom sat down beside me on the bench. I'd been so lost in my memories of Blake that I hadn't even heard her come in, but I scooted over to give her room.

"You've been practicing minor scales for twenty minutes," she said. "Must've been a really, really bad day." The piano had belonged to Grandma before she'd given it to us, and Mom had taken years of lessons when she was my age, though she rarely played anymore.

I shrugged.

"Does it have anything to do with you and Blake?"

I nodded.

"Did you apologize like we talked about?"

"It didn't help." Talking about him tore open the wound. "Blake's different."

"People change as they get older." Mom looped her arm around my shoulders. "You're changing too."

"I don't want to."

"It's part of life, Hector. People change, and friends sometimes grow apart."

"But it's like someone flipped a switch and made Blake into an entirely different person. Even when he was angry before, he was never mean."

"Hector, you're more sensitive and—"

"I am not!"

Mom let go of me and leaned back to look me in the eye. "Baby, you are, and that's okay! If everyone was as sensitive as you, the world would be a kinder place. But most people are more like—"

"Pop and the boys?"

Mom smiled. "Exactly. And that's not a bad thing either. It just means life is going to be a little more difficult for you."

"That doesn't seem fair."

Mom lowered her head. "It's not."

It wasn't the answer I was hoping for, but I appreciated her honesty. "Do you ever wish I was different? More like Jason or Lee?"

"Not for a second."

"Are you sure?"

"You've always known who you are," Mom said, "and I admire that about you."

"You do?"

Mom nodded. "But not everyone has your certainty. Some people struggle to find themselves, and some never do."

"Do you think that's what Blake's doing?" Blake had always seemed confident to me before. Maybe it had been an act.

Mom leaned into me and smiled. "I don't know, but if anyone can get through to him, it's you."

Despite what Mom said, I didn't feel certain. I felt alone and confused and scared that I'd lost my best friend forever. Eventually, I returned to my scales. Mom sat beside me while I played, and listened.

# 11

MR. MORHILL SET the stack of books on the table where I was rushing through the social studies worksheet I hadn't finished the night before. "What do octopi, light, camouflage, ghosts, and five years' worth of school yearbooks have in common?"

I finished the last question, pushed the worksheet aside, and looked up. "What?"

"I don't know, Mr. Griggs. That's why I asked *you.*"

Since Mr. Morhill already believed St. Lawrence's was haunted, I didn't think there was any harm telling him about Orson. "I ran into the ghost again, I think. I actually saw it this time. Him, I mean. He spoke to me, *and* he was dressed like a student." The more I considered it, the more likely it seemed that Orson Wellington and the ghost were one and the same.

Mr. Morhill patted the yearbooks. "So you intend to comb through these in an attempt to ascertain his identity?"

"I already know his name. Orson Wellington. He ran off before I could learn more."

Mr. Morhill pulled out a chair and sat down, chewing over what I'd said. "Then why do you need the yearbooks?"

"To find out if he was really a student here and, if so, when. Maybe I can ask some of the teachers what happened to him."

"Surely, if some tragedy befell the young man which rendered him an apparition, you could unearth the circumstances using the computer."

I rolled my eyes. "I already searched his name online. Zero results."

"With a unique name like Orson Wellington, you should have easily discovered the circumstances behind his demise if they existed."

"Exactly."

"Clever, Mr. Griggs." He glanced at the stack of books again. "That explains the yearbooks. What about these others?"

Explaining those was going to be tricky. I was a terrible liar, but I wasn't ready to give up my secret about turning invisible. I was trying to decide what to tell Mr. Morhill when I spied my reflection in a window and had an idea. "What if the ghost isn't actually a ghost?"

Mr. Morhill's eyebrows rose. "I'm intrigued. Go on."

"Well, if something bad happened to him, it would've

been in the news and I would've found it online, right? So what if he's not a ghost?" *What if he's like me?* "What if we just can't see him?"

"Intriguing hypothesis." Mr. Morhill rubbed his chin.

I was still groping around in the dark for answers, but if anyone could help me figure out what was happening, Mr. Morhill could. "What if Orson Wellington is invisible, but most people can't hear him, and he can't touch anything? Except doors."

"Why doors?"

I shrugged.

Mr. Morhill wrinkled his nose. "What you've described certainly sounds like we're dealing with an incorporeal ghost."

"Incor-what?"

"Incorporeal," Mr. Morhill repeated. "Insubstantial."

"Oh. So when is a ghost not really a ghost?"

A group of younger boys entered the library. They looked like they'd wound up there by accident or on a dare. Mr. Morhill rose. "Pardon me a moment, Hector."

While Mr. Morhill was away, I flipped through the yearbooks, beginning with the most recent and working backward. Orson wasn't in the first, or the second. It was the worst game of *Where's Waldo?* ever. But when I opened the yearbook from three years ago, I found him staring back at me from the group photo of the 7W class. He looked exactly the same as he had in the stairwell, though less terrified. I returned to the yearbook from two years ago to search for him in the eighth-grade section but didn't find him. Which meant that whatever had happened to him must have occurred between two and three years ago.

"You really like yearbooks, huh?"

I stifled a yelp and looked up to find a girl standing beside my table. She was taller than me, with long brown hair pulled back in a ponytail, mischievous eyes, braces, and a galaxy of freckles. I'd had plenty of girls as friends when I went to public school, but unless something had changed that I wasn't aware of, girls weren't allowed to attend St. Lawrence's.

"You're not supposed to be here," I blurted out.

She cocked her head to the side. "Why? Is this a secret library? Am I wearing the uniform wrong?"

"Because this is a boys' school!"

She frowned, and creases lined her forehead. She quickly shook them off and said, "If you keep my secret, I won't tell anyone about your yearbook obsession." She flashed a smile. "I'm Samantha Osborne. Everyone calls me Sam."

There was something intimidating about Sam's easy confidence that threw me off balance. I wanted to ask her about her secret, but I could only manage to spit out my name. "Hector Griggs."

"Hector?"

"My mom's kind of obsessed with Greek mythology."

Sam rolled my name around on her tongue like it was an unfamiliar food and she was trying to decide if she liked the taste. Finally she nodded. "It's a good name."

56

"Thanks, I guess."

Sam shrugged and said, "Well, you're clearly busy, so I'll leave you to it," and disappeared around the corner.

As soon as Sam was gone, I thought of all the things I should have said. I'd been the new student once, so I knew how lonely it was, and I could've been more welcoming. I considered chasing after Sam to apologize, but the bell rang for us to assemble outside for homeroom. I grabbed the yearbook with Orson Wellington's picture in it and took it to Mr. Morhill at the circulation desk so he could make a photocopy. It would have been easier if I could have taken a picture of it with my phone, but students weren't allowed to carry phones on campus.

While I waited for Mr. Morhill to copy the page from the yearbook, Sam waved from the door and said, "See you around, Hector."

Mr. Morhill handed me my photocopy. "My niece. She's in seventh grade, but I was hoping you two would meet."

"But there aren't supposed to be any girls at St. Lawrence's, right?"

"Then it might be best if you don't mention it to anyone else." Mr. Morhill winked and sent me on my way.

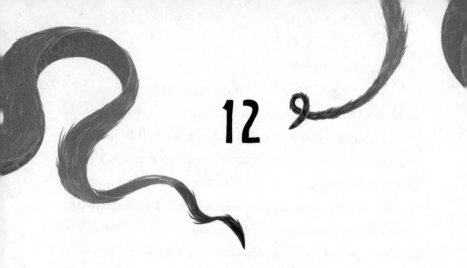

# 12

AS FAR AS I could tell, I was the only person other than Mr. Morhill who recognized that Sam Osborne was a girl. She was in seventh grade, so I wasn't in classes with her, but I would have heard about it if anyone else had noticed. A girl at St. Lawrence's would've been the biggest news since someone found out Mr. Grady had been in a punk rock band before he'd become a teacher. He refused to talk about it, but there were videos on YouTube. No one was talking about Sam, though.

Sam was a mystery, but not the mystery I needed to focus on. That honor belonged to Orson Wellington.

After science, I hung back to talk to Colonel Musser. She was the homeroom teacher for the 7W class and had been for years. If Orson had been in her class, she would recognize him.

"Problem, Hector?" she asked.

Students frequently whispered mean jokes about Colonel Musser—about her short hair, the clothes she wore, and the fact that she rode a motorcycle to school—but I didn't think they were funny. Musser was honest, she treated every question like it was important and tried to answer it to the best of her ability, and she wasn't afraid to admit when she didn't know something. After Mr. Morhill, Colonel Musser was my favorite teacher.

I didn't have much time before my next class, and the 8E students were already trickling into Musser's room, so I spit out my question. "Do you remember a student named Orson Wellington?"

As Colonel Musser frowned, the space between her eyes wrinkled. "Can't say that I do."

"He would've been in your homeroom three years ago."

"I know I'm old, but my memory isn't so soft that I wouldn't remember a name like Orson Wellington. You must be mistaken." Musser turned to the whiteboard to wipe it clean.

I pulled out the photocopied yearbook page and handed it to her.

"What is it that you want me to look at?"

I pointed at Orson. "That's him. Orson Wellington. See?"

"See who?" Musser's right eyebrow lifted sharply. "I don't know what game you're playing, Hector, but I am not amused."

"Don't you see him? He's right there."

The warning bell rang. "You best get to class."

I didn't know how she didn't see Orson in the picture, but I did know it was pointless to argue. I reached for the photocopy. Colonel Musser held on to it tightly and gave me the eyebrow.

I ran into social studies as the final bell rang and slid into my seat. How could Musser not have recognized Orson? She'd joked about her memory, but I bet she remembered the name of every student who'd ever sat in her class for as long as she'd been teaching at St. Lawrence's. And she'd been there a long time. When I'd shown her the page, though, it wasn't like she didn't recognize him. It was like she hadn't been able to see him at all.

I'd have to ask Mr. Morhill to make another photocopy so I could show it to a few other teachers. One of them would remember Orson Wellington. I hoped.

At lunch, I planned to sneak away to practice being invisible and look for Orson, but Sam Osborne fell in beside me at the cafeteria and latched on.

"What's good to eat here?"

"Uh, it's Thursday," I said.

Sam screwed up her face, confused. "Okay?"

"Never, ever eat cafeteria lunch on Thursdays unless you want to spend the rest of the afternoon sick."

Understanding dawned on Sam's face. "Thanks for the tip. It would've been nice if Uncle Archie had mentioned it. Now what am I going to eat for lunch?"

*Archie?* She couldn't have been talking about Mr.

Morhill. He certainly didn't look like an Archie. Since I doubted I'd be able to ditch Sam without being rude, I held up my lunch bag. "I have a peanut butter and jelly sandwich and a pack of Nutty Buddy bars. I'll share them with you if you want."

Sam chucked me playfully in the shoulder. "Deal! I can buy some Tater Tots to go with the PB and J. Are the tots okay to eat?"

"The tots are good."

"Then I'll find you at the table." Sam took off to get in line.

I picked a spot at the end of my regular table with the cupcakes and was unpacking my lunch when Sam rolled up. She sat across from me and set the basket of Tater Tots between us. Sam turned to the left and waved. "Hey, I'm Sam."

I watched to see if anyone at the table noticed Sam was a girl, but no one seemed to. It was possible I could have made a mistake—it wasn't as if boys couldn't have long hair, except at St. Lawrence's, where our hair had to be off our collars—but Mr. Morhill had specifically said she was his niece. I wished we were alone so I could ask her why no one else seemed to recognize she was a girl.

"That's Paul," I said, pointing to the boy beside her, who was too busy playing his Switch under the table to do anything more than grunt. "The one with the book is Trevor, across from him is Jackson, and down at the end is Mike."

"Matt," he called without looking up from his homework.

"Sorry," I said. "Matt."

Sam lowered her voice. "Are they your friends?"

"They're not *not* my friends."

"He only sits with us because he hasn't got anywhere else to go," Paul said. It was the most I'd ever heard him speak, even though we were in the same homeroom. Matt was a sixth grader too. Jackson and Trevor were in seventh.

Sam looked curious but didn't ask what Paul meant. I shoved her half of my lunch across the table. "This school's weird," Sam said.

I shrugged. "You get used to it."

Sam plucked at her shirt. "What's with the uniforms? Couldn't they have at least picked better colors?"

Without looking up from his Switch, Paul said, "I've made the same complaint to Principal O'Shea every year. Who pairs canary yellow with khaki? But do you think he listens?"

"At least we don't have to worry about what to wear in the morning," I said.

Sam seemed to consider my argument. "Fine, but what's the deal with Colonel Musser? Was she in the army? I don't get it."

I shook my head. "It's just a nickname. She's tough, but pretty cool."

While we ate, I filled Sam in on the other teachers. "Mr. Grady never checks the homework, so it doesn't matter if the answers are wrong as long as you turn it in on time."

Jackson added, "And when you write him essays, he cares more about grammar, spelling, and punctuation than the topic."

"True," I said.

Sam nodded along like she was mentally taking notes.

"Mrs. Ford—"

"Don't mess with her at all," Matt shouted from the end of the table.

"She loves to pick on students," I said.

Paul said, "I heard she got bullied when she was our age and now she gets her revenge by bullying us."

"I believe it," Trevor said.

I didn't know what it was about Sam that had made the other boys so talkative. They'd barely acknowledged my existence before. "Okay, but she's nothing compared to Coach Barbary."

The other boys nodded sagely.

Paul had put his Switch away and turned to us. "I don't know what his problem is."

"He hates kids," Matt called.

"Nah," Jackson said. "He's got his favorites."

"Thanks for being so nice," Sam said. "It sucks being dumped in a new school after the year's already started."

All at once, the other boys quit talking and looked away. They were like turtles withdrawing into their shells. I didn't realize why until I turned and saw Blake, Evan, and Conrad Eldridge approaching.

Blake snatched my half-eaten Nutty Buddy bar off the table and took a bite before turning to Sam. "You're new here, right?" he said, spraying crumbs. "I'm Blake Nesbitt."

"Sam Osborne," she said cautiously.

Blake motioned at the table. "You shouldn't sit with the cupcakes. No one here but losers. Especially Hector."

Conrad whispered into Blake's ear, and Blake laughed.

"Something funny?" Sam asked.

"Just be careful who you sit with. Don't want people getting the wrong idea about you."

A friendly, almost grateful smile hit Sam's lips. "Thanks for the heads-up, but I don't care what people think of me."

Blake leaned in. "Maybe you should."

Sam shrugged. "There are an awful lot of people in the world, and if I worried about all their opinions of me, I wouldn't have time for anything else."

"You don't have to care what everyone thinks," Blake said. "Only people who matter."

Sam snorted, barely holding back a laugh. "And you think that's *you*?"

"Well, yeah. Duh."

"Okay," Sam said. "Sure." She turned away from the boys and back to me.

Blake stood with his mouth open, staring at Sam for a moment before storming off and taking Evan and Conrad with him.

"Cupcakes?" Sam said when Blake was gone.

Paul rolled his eyes. "That's what people call us."

"Why? I love cupcakes."

"They think it's an insult," Trevor said. "And they know they won't get in trouble for using it like they would if they called us something worse. I don't even know who started it."

"This school is really strange."

The other boys nodded their agreement and then retreated back to their bubbles. It was like Blake had sucked all the fun out of lunch. We ate in awkward silence until Sam said, "That Blake guy really doesn't like you, does he, Hector?"

"He used to be my best friend."

Sam's eyebrows rose. "You were friends with that jerk?"

"He wasn't always like that."

"Really? What happened?"

Seeing Sam stand up to Blake made me want to trust her. If nothing else, maybe she could help me understand why he hated me. "I asked Blake to be my boyfriend, he called me a bad name and said we weren't friends anymore, and I set fire to his science project."

"No offense, Hector, but I'd be pretty upset if you set *my* project on fire."

"It was a really bad name." When Sam still didn't look convinced, I leaned across the table and whispered it into her ear.

"Oh!" Sam said, her eyes wide. "Okay. Yeah. I mean, I still don't think setting his stuff on fire was right, but I get it."

"I tried to apologize, but he won't talk to me. We even got into a fight. A real one." I didn't want to cry with the other boys around, because it might get back to Jason, who'd tell Pop, and then Pop would say boys shouldn't cry, so I scrubbed my eyes with my hand.

"I'm sorry, Hector," Sam said.

"It's just, Blake was never mean before. It feels like someone stole my best friend and replaced him with a monster."

Sam cocked her head to the side and shrugged. "Who knows? Maybe someone did."

# 13

FRIDAY, I ASKED Mr. Morhill to photocopy the page of the yearbook with Orson Wellington's picture again, and I showed it to some of the other teachers. Mr. Grady glanced at the picture but ignored my question, Ms. Martinez asked me why I was wasting her time, and I didn't bother asking Mrs. Ford, because she wouldn't have told me even if she did remember him. They all reacted the way Musser had. They didn't recognize his name and couldn't see his picture. It was strange, and I couldn't explain it.

I was sitting in Mrs. Gallagher's class, trying to figure out who else I could ask about Orson, when I had an idea. Maybe the solution to learning more about Orson Wellington was to find him and ask him directly. I hadn't forgotten how something had scared him away last time. "Don't cry," he'd said. "Crying attracts *it*." I didn't know what *it* was, and

I didn't want to, but finding Orson and learning more about him was worth the risk.

"Mrs. Gallagher?" I raised my hand as high as I could. Mrs. Gallagher was nearly eighty, and it took a little extra work to grab her attention. "May I use the restroom?"

Most teachers were strict with the restroom pass, but Mrs. Gallagher let anyone go who needed it and didn't keep track of how long they were gone. I could probably stay out the rest of class and she wouldn't notice—not that I planned to be gone that long. Sure enough, Mrs. Gallagher nodded that I could go, and I took off.

I hadn't turned invisible since seeing Orson in the stairwell, and I was a little afraid I wouldn't be able to do it again, but as soon as I shut the door behind me, I only had to think about it and I vanished. It was as easy as passing out of a sunbeam into a shadow. Exhilaration lifted me like a helium-filled balloon. I felt invincible.

"Hello?" I called. "Orson?" I looked around the hallway, but it was empty, so I headed toward the stairwell where I first ran into him. "Orson Wellington?"

If he was around, he wasn't answering.

It was thrilling to be invisible. I could run screaming through the school, and no one could see or hear me. I could walk into any classroom and no one would know I was there. Maybe, with my power, I'd become a spy. I could infiltrate impenetrable buildings, get close to people no other spy could reach. The possibilities were endless!

I treated finding Orson like a secret mission. I crept

downstairs to the first floor and peered through windows into classrooms. I checked the infirmary and the mail room. I even peeked into the teachers' lounge, which was a letdown. It was only a boring room with a couple of old couches, a table, a coffee maker, a microwave, and a mini-fridge that hummed loudly.

Before returning to class, I stopped by the principal's office. Miss DeVore, Principal O'Shea's secretary, sat at her desk in the small waiting room outside the office, typing on her computer. She was a sweet old woman who always offered kind words and candy to the boys waiting to see Principal O'Shea, even if they were there because they'd gotten in trouble. Students joked that she'd been around as long as the school itself, and I believed it. She was definitely older than either of my grandmas.

"Orson? You here?"

Miss DeVore stopped typing and looked up. She took off her thick glasses and let them hang from the chain around her neck. No one else had been able to hear me while I was invisible, but I stood silently, too afraid to move. Finally she chuckled, put her glasses back on, and returned to her work.

Slowly, I crept out of the office and headed back to class. As I was climbing the stairs to the second floor, I heard a noise behind me, a thumping beat. I paused at the railing and looked down as Orson Wellington burst into the stairwell. Sweat soaked his face, and his glasses were crooked. He spotted me standing there and screamed, "Run!"

The terror in his voice triggered a reflex, and I ran. Orson flew up the steps so quickly that he was at my back, pushing and shoving me into the hall before I'd gone two steps. I turned to ask him what was happening, but I forgot how to speak when I saw *it*.

A long, grizzled tentacle snaked up the stairs toward us. Clusters of wiry hair poked out of mottled green flesh, and instead of suckers, the pale underside was dotted with gaping mouths filled with needle teeth. I couldn't see the body the tentacle was attached to, and I hoped I never did. It looked like something that had crawled out of a nightmare, but it was worse than a nightmare because I couldn't wake up.

I screamed and tripped over my feet. As I fell, I got tangled with Orson, and we both hit the floor.

"Move!" Orson's voice cracked as he freed himself from the knot of arms and legs I'd created.

I flipped over onto my butt and crab-crawled away from the monster as far and as fast as possible.

The tentacle reared in the air. Its many mouths smacked their lips and bared their sharp teeth. I could smell it, rotting and putrid, like the food in our fridge after a hurricane had killed our power for a few days. The tentacle lashed out and wrapped around my ankle. One of the mouths attached to my skin. I screamed in pain, kicking the monster and clawing at the floor to get free.

In my panic, I attempted to turn visible. The hallway flickered. For a second I could see through the tentacle before it solidified once more. The tentacle tightened its grip on my ankle, squeezing me tighter than an unwanted hug from Aunt Claire. I tried to turn visible again, but nothing happened. Not even a glimmer.

That was it. I was going to be eaten by a monstrous tentacle with teeth. Mom would always wonder what had happened to me, Blake would never know how sorry I was, and Jason would finally get our room to himself and would definitely call dibs on all my best stuff. I didn't want to die, but I couldn't break free.

As the tentacle dragged me into the stairwell, Orson ran toward me, his glasses askew, yelling like his hair was on fire. He stabbed a pair of scissors into the meaty tentacle holding me captive. A hundred toothy mouths shrieked in unison, and the tentacle loosened its grip on my ankle enough for me to escape.

"Run!" Orson shouted again.

I leapt to my feet, turning visible without thinking, and ran right into a door as Colonel Musser stepped into the hallway. I bounced off the door and smacked into the wall, feeling like a pinball.

"Hector Griggs! What in the world are you doing in this hallway screaming like a banshee?" Musser's right eyebrow was raised higher than I'd ever seen it.

Mr. Grady and Ms. Gonzalez had also stuck their heads into the hall to investigate.

"There's a monster—" I said, forgetting I was visible in the confusion, only realizing when I turned around that the tentacle and Orson Wellington were gone.

# 14

THERE WAS A monster at the school. All I'd seen of it was a single tentacle with toothy mouths instead of suckers, and I had zero desire to see the rest. The spot on my ankle where the monster had bitten me throbbed with my heartbeat. There hadn't been a wound when I'd pulled up my pants leg to show Colonel Musser, but it had been real. The monster was real. Orson Wellington was real, and I'd left him alone.

The teachers must've heard me screaming when I'd tried to turn visible during my flight from the monster. I didn't understand how, but the monster had prevented me from fleeing, and I had no doubt it would have eaten me if Orson hadn't come to my rescue. I'd repaid his bravery by running away. I hoped he'd managed to escape. I might've turned invisible to check on him, but I had other problems.

"Sneaking around school? Making up ludicrous stories

about monsters and ghosts and invisible boys? And I hear from Coach Barbary that you've been fighting with Blake Nesbitt?" Principal O'Shea laced his bony fingers together and rested them on the desk. "What has gotten into you, Hector?"

Principal O'Shea was possibly the oldest man I'd met in my entire life. Wispy white hair stuck out from behind and inside his ears, his papery skin was spotted and gray, and his thick glasses gave him bug eyes. Usually, he was kind, ready with a silly joke, but he wasn't armed with jokes today.

"I didn't make up the story!" I said. "There was a monster! *And* a boy named Orson—"

"Enough!" My mom, sitting in the chair beside me, smacked the armrest with her palm. "No more lies!"

I knew the situation was grim when Principal O'Shea had called my mom. She'd arrived wearing a scowl that looked like it had been chiseled onto her stony face. When she and Principal O'Shea had demanded to know why I was in the hallway, I'd taken a chance and told the truth. The students and teachers deserved to know they were sharing their school with a monster and that none of us were safe. I hadn't expected Principal O'Shea to believe me, but Mom knew I didn't like to lie *and* that I wasn't very good at it. I didn't know what I could say that wouldn't make the situation worse, so I hung my head and kept quiet.

Principal O'Shea sighed. "It seems to me that Gene has the fighting situation well in hand, but there must be consequences for sneaking out of class and causing a ruckus."

Mom snorted and said, "There will definitely be consequences." Her tone made her almost as scary as the monster.

"I believe a week of lunch detention will teach you a valuable lesson."

I half stood. "A week?"

Principal O'Shea continued as if I hadn't spoken. "You'll begin Monday. Miss DeVore has plenty of tasks to keep your idle hands busy."

I sank back into my seat, feeling miserable. Mom and Pop and my teachers were always talking about the importance of honesty, but I'd told the truth, and all it had gotten me was detention.

Principal O'Shea tilted his head and offered a sincere smile. "Chin up, Hector. It's not the end of the world. Keep your nose clean, and in a week this incident will be behind you."

"Yes, sir," I mumbled.

Principal O'Shea seemed satisfied the situation was settled, but my mom was just getting warmed up. She'd decided it would be easier to take me home for the rest of the day so Pop wouldn't have to drop me off before taking Jason to baseball. It was the first time I actually wished I could stay at school. Thankfully, Mom waited until we were in the car to let me have it. She didn't yell, though, which made it so much worse.

"I'm disappointed in you, Hector. I was in the middle of a meeting when your school called. Do you know how embarrassing it is to explain to a client that I need to reschedule because my son was found skipping class and telling stories about a monster?"

Mom gripped the steering wheel tightly in her bloodless hands. She glanced at me in the rearview mirror when she reached a stoplight.

"What were you thinking, Hector?"

"I—"

"And if you mention monsters or ghosts, I will cancel your lessons and sell the piano."

My lip trembled. It was all I could do not to cry. "You said I could tell you anything. That you'd always listen to me, always believe me. Well, I'm telling the truth. Why won't you believe me now?"

"Enough." Mom's voice snapped like a wet towel. "No more video games, no more internet, no more TV."

I wasn't getting through to her, and trying was only making her angrier. "Yes, ma'am."

"I'll have chores for you to do after school. When you're not studying or practicing piano, you'll work around the house. That includes weekends."

"For how long?" I asked.

"Until I'm not disappointed in you anymore or you finally decide to quit telling lies."

It would have been easier if she'd just said "forever."

# 15

MOM KEPT HER word. I barely slept Friday night because every time I closed my eyes, I saw the toothy tentacle looming over me. Sometimes it squeezed me until I couldn't breathe; other times it dragged me into the darkness where I couldn't see anything. When I *did* fall asleep, I woke up drenched in sweat from nightmares. But none of that mattered to Mom. She hauled me out of bed early Saturday and handed me a list of the dirtiest, nastiest chores she could think of.

"Careful," Jason said from behind me while I was in the bathroom cleaning the tile grout with a toothbrush. "Don't want the monster to get you!" He fake screamed as Lee pounced from behind and carried him away.

They were like that all weekend, exploiting every opportunity to make fun of me. The only person who offered me any sympathy was Pop, which was a surprise.

Sunday afternoon Mom set me to pulling weeds around

the yard while Pop was mowing the grass. It was hot, even in the shade, and I was grateful when Pop showed up with a couple of glasses of iced tea.

"I used to tell stories when I was your age," Pop said. "Real whoppers."

I'd given up trying to convince them I wasn't lying.

"This one time, I told everyone at school that my parents had been criminals and that we were in hiding from the mob."

That didn't sound like Pop at all. "You did?"

Pop nodded. "I wanted people to like me, and I figured I needed to be more interesting, so I made up a bunch of stories. But you know what happened?"

"They found out?"

"Yup," Pop said. "I told so many stories that I couldn't remember who I'd told what, and then everyone called me a liar. It took a long time to escape that reputation."

"Oh."

I wanted to tell Pop that I wasn't lying, and I wasn't trying to make people like me, but I doubted that would make a difference.

Pop rested his hand on my shoulder. "Your mom loves you, kiddo. Go easy on her, okay? Cut it out with the lies, and this will blow over."

It was rare for Pop to talk to me like this, and I thought maybe he'd be willing to listen. "What if I'm not lying?"

Pop glanced at me. "About there being a monster and a ghost at your school?"

"Yeah."

"I hope you *are* lying, Hector," he said. "Because if you actually believe that nonsense, then you need the kind of help your mom and I can't give you."

I didn't know exactly what Pop meant, but it sounded less like help and more like a threat. If I couldn't convince anyone I was telling the truth about what I'd seen, then that meant I would have to face it on my own.

# 16

MONDAY MORNING, I sat in the music room inside the library playing one of my favorite songs on the piano. Mr. Morhill had been busy when I'd come in, which I was grateful for because I wasn't in the mood to talk to anyone. All weekend, I'd been dreading what was waiting for me at school. Not just Orson and the monster, but everyone who'd heard me screaming in the hallway. I hoped I could get through the day without being beaten up or made fun of or attacked by a giant, toothy tentacle.

I was surprised when Sam walked into the music room and sat down behind an ancient drum kit. At first I thought she was just going to listen, but she grabbed the sticks and quickly picked up the rhythm of the song. We played together for a few minutes, and I lost myself in the music. I forgot about my fingers that ached from scrubbing toilets and pulling weeds, about Orson Wellington, about the monster. Until we reached the end of the song.

"That was nice," Sam said. "What is it?"

"It's from a video game my mom says I'm not old enough to play yet. I stumbled across a recording of a Japanese musician doing a jazzy cover of it and fell in love." I glanced at Sam. "You're a drummer?"

"Sometimes." She twirled a drumstick around her right hand.

"Show-off."

"Guilty." Sam stared at me like she was waiting for me to say something, but I didn't know what. "So, are you going to tell me what happened Friday or should I start guessing?"

I turned back to the piano and pretended to study my sheet music.

"Right," Sam said. "You were in the restroom when a giant rat crawled out of the toilet and chased you down the hall." She paused. "No? Okay. You slipped in a puddle, cracked your head on the sink, and found yourself in a parallel world where everyone spoke bad French."

Without looking up, I said, "Blake was right. You should find someone else to be friends with."

"Uncle Archie says St. Lawrence's is haunted," Sam said, ignoring my suggestion. "Did you see the ghost? Is that what scared you?"

I didn't want to talk about the ghost with Sam, so I tried to change the subject. "Is Mr. Morhill's first name really Archie?"

"Archibald Tarquin Morhill. Archie for short."

"And I thought Hector was bad," I muttered.

"So, the ghost." Sam wasn't going to give up easily.

"The ghost isn't . . . I mean, it's not . . ." I shook my head. "You wouldn't believe me."

"Sorry to disappoint you, but we haven't been friends long enough for you to know what I'd believe." She counted off on her fingers. "I believe in aliens, ghosts, the multiverse. Sometimes I have dreams about things that come true. I'm pretty sure magic is real, but I'm not sure if it's actual magic or just science we don't understand yet."

I wanted to talk to someone about what I'd seen. I *needed* to talk to someone. The problem was that I didn't know Sam that well yet. She'd been nice to me so far, and she'd stood up to Blake, but what if she thought I was a liar like everyone else did? At the same time, Orson was still out there. I didn't know if he was a ghost or invisible like me, but he was alone with a monster. I owed it to him to at least make sure he was alive. Unless he really was a ghost, in which case I guessed being eaten wouldn't matter. Either way, Sam might be able to help. I didn't know what to do.

"You can trust me," Sam said.

Before I could make a decision, the bell rang. I gathered my music, stuffed it in my bag, and headed outside to join the 6W class at the back of the line. Mr. Grady led us inside. The closer we got to the stairwell, the heavier my feet felt. I could smell the monster; I could hear its shriek when Orson had stabbed it. The invisible wound on my ankle pulsed faster. I felt like I couldn't breathe. How was I ever going to find Orson when I couldn't even climb the stairs?

No. I could do this. I took the steps two at a time and reached the top floor.

"Monster!" Blake jumped out at me as I came out of the stairwell.

I screamed and fell sideways. I nearly became invisible from the fright before I realized I was surrounded by a group of sixth, seventh, and eighth graders. Blake was holding his side from laughing. Conrad Eldridge whispered something in his ear that made Blake crack up even harder.

The wall of boys fell as Colonel Musser approached. "Enough of this foolishness. Everyone, get to class."

I marched to Mr. Grady's classroom, ignoring the snickers that followed me.

- - - - - -

Running for Coach Barbary was getting a little easier each day. I wasn't breathing as hard as I had been the week before. Blake was still faster, and he could have left me behind, but he jogged beside me instead, making it difficult to put him out of my mind.

"Conrad Eldridge?" I said.

Blake kept his eyes forward. "What about him?"

"You're friends with eighth graders now?"

"Not all of us are babies crying about seeing monsters that don't exist."

"The monster is real," I said. "I don't care if you don't believe me."

"Sure."

Running and talking at the same time was a challenge. I took a couple of seconds to catch my breath before asking another question. "What's Conrad always whispering to you?"

"Stuff."

"What kind of stuff?"

"Stuff you wouldn't understand."

"Why not?" I asked.

"Because you're a *freak*."

The word felt like a punch. "Stop calling me that."

"Why?" Blake said. "You are one."

"What would your moms say if they heard you use that word?"

Blake stumbled, and for half a second I could see my old friend in his eyes. But his expression vanished quickly, replaced by a sneer. "Go on and tell. Not like anyone would believe you, since you love telling lies."

I wished I could hate Blake, but I also wished I could have my best friend back. It was confusing to love someone so much and despise them at the same time.

"If there is a monster here, maybe you should do everyone a favor and let it eat you." In a lower voice, almost a whisper, Blake said, "It's gonna win either way."

I pulled Blake's sleeve, yanking him to a stop so he had to face me. "You know something! Have you seen it? What is it?"

There was something wrong with Blake. His skin was flushed and his eyes were glassy and bloodshot. He looked feverish and sick, like he had the flu.

"It's . . ." Blake grimaced. Sweat dripped from the hair hanging in his eyes. He glanced over his shoulder toward the school, then back at me. "I don't know what you're talking about, *freak.*" He shoved me and started running again.

I looked toward the main building, scanning the windows. There on the second floor, peering out of Mrs. Ford's classroom, was Conrad Eldridge.

**17**

FOR MY FIRST lunch detention, Miss DeVore had me sitting in a chair beside her desk stuffing and sealing envelopes. She let me eat my sandwich and wash my hands before I began so I wouldn't get any mustard on the letters. It wasn't the worst punishment I'd ever endured, and it was certainly better than pulling weeds.

"You remind me of another young man who passed through this school many years ago," Miss DeVore said. She had a seemingly endless treasure trove of stories about St. Lawrence students.

"Who?"

"Back then he was called Ulysses, though these days he goes by Gene. You know him as—"

"Coach Barbary? I remind you of Coach Barbary?" I wasn't sure whether she meant it as an insult or not.

Miss DeVore smiled. She had a smudge of red lipstick

on her gray teeth. "He was a quiet, shy child. Always with his head in the clouds. The way he told stories, I assumed he would grow up to write fantastic novels."

I was having a tough time seeing Coach Barbary as a storyteller. "I figured he was born with that whistle around his neck."

Miss DeVore chuckled. "I assure you, the man who referees your sports games isn't the same boy who used to hide in the infirmary with a tummy ache to avoid the other students."

"He was bullied?"

Miss DeVore nodded. "He had sticky fingers too, if I recall correctly."

"Really?"

"Items that went missing seemed to find their way into his pockets," Miss DeVore said. "Why, I remember he was even caught with Helena's wedding ring. That's Mrs. Gallagher to you. Ulysses claimed that he'd found it and was going to return it to her, but he refused to say *where* he'd found it."

So Coach Barbary had been a victim of bullies, a liar, *and* a thief? "How did Coach wind up back here?"

Miss DeVore scooped up the stack of envelopes I'd stuffed and bound them together with a rubber band. "People change, Hector. They grow up. They grow old. The things they believe become things they're embarrassed they once considered true. A person can live many lives over the course of one life." She sounded wistful and a bit sad, but I didn't understand why.

"Like how my mom wanted to be a concert pianist when she was younger but now she works with computers?"

"Something like that," Miss DeVore said. "But young Ulysses's change was more than the casualty of a dream. He lost a friend, if I remember correctly. A best friend."

I thought of Blake, and the pain from his words hurt all over again.

"When you find people who accept you as you are, Hector, hold on to them. Fight for them, even if it feels hopeless." Miss DeVore fell silent, her eyes looking into the distance. A moment later, she shook her head and chuckled. "My apologies. Missing lunch is punishment enough. You shouldn't have to suffer maudlin stories from an old lady with a long memory."

"I don't mind," I said. "Were any of the other teachers students here?"

"No," Miss DeVore said. "But I knew Tabitha Ford's mother. We had our hair fixed at the same salon. Apparently, Tabitha was quite the troublemaker when she was your age."

"Mrs. Ford's name is Tabitha?"

"Indeed. But she wasn't a Ford back then. She was Tabitha Pendleton. And I seem to recall hearing about an incident with a pig that ended with the police being telephoned."

The bell rang, and I was actually disappointed for detention to end—I would've loved to get some dirt on Mrs. Ford—but what Miss DeVore had said, about finding people who accept you, stuck in my head. Blake might not have wanted to be my friend anymore, but Sam did. I'd never know if I could trust her if I didn't give her the chance. I dashed off to talk to her before she got to her classroom.

"Why are you so sweaty?" Sam asked. "What in the world were you doing during detention?"

The warning bell rang. "Sorry about this morning. I want to tell you what happened. If you still want to know."

"Get to class, Hector," Colonel Musser called.

Sam pursed her lips thoughtfully. Finally she nodded once. "Meet me at the library after school."

"I can't," I said. "Pop will be waiting for me, and he hates if I'm late."

Sam said, "I'll take care of it. Just meet me."

- - - - - -

Mr. Morhill smiled when I walked into the library after last period. "I'm happy to give you a ride home so you and Sam can work on your project," he said.

I was a little confused. "You are?"

"Certainly," Mr. Morhill said. "And I've already spoken to your mom—lovely woman—and cleared it with her." He pointed toward the back. "Sam's waiting for you."

I found Sam right where Mr. Morhill had indicated. I set my bag down and sat, nervous to begin. "Did you arrange that with your uncle?"

"So we have plenty of time to talk." When I hesitated, Sam said, "Whatever it is, I'll believe you." Her sincerity put me at ease.

"The ghost is real," I said. "Except I'm not sure he's actually a ghost. He's a student named Orson Wellington. At least, he *was* a student three years ago."

I paused, waiting for Sam to tell me I was making it up or that I had a vivid imagination, but she sat patiently, listening.

"So it all began last week when I was running from Blake and I heard a voice." I told Sam about the clergy house, about turning invisible in the church, about finding Orson Wellington, and about being attacked by the tentacle monster.

"And somehow, I think what's happening with Blake is connected. He's been hanging out with this eighth grader, Conrad Eldridge, and he seems scared of him. Once, when I asked him why he wouldn't stop bullying me, he said because *he* wouldn't let him. Creepy, right?"

"Totally," Sam said. "Can I see you turn invisible? Not because I don't believe you. I'm just curious how it works."

The last time I'd done it was when I'd seen the monster in the stairwell, and I'd been too scared to try again since. I was terrified the monster would be waiting for me, but I was as safe here in the library with Sam as anywhere, so I shut my eyes and vanished. Sam didn't look nearly as surprised as I'd expected her to. If someone had disappeared in front of me, I probably would have fallen out of my seat.

I only stayed invisible for a couple of seconds before turning visible again.

"That's seriously cool, and I have so many questions." Sam reached into her backpack and pulled out a notebook and pen. "But Orson Wellington and the monster should be our first priority." She opened to a blank page and began writing.

1. Ghost named Orson Wellington. Former student? Actual ghost? Invisible boy?
2. Monster. Tentacles. Lots of teeth. Natural or *super*natural?
3. Blake Nesbitt. Monster, being controlled by a monster, or just a jerk?
4. Hector's invisibility. Is he actually turning invisible or is it something else?

I pointed to Sam's fourth entry. "You saw me do it with your own eyes."

"But you said no one could hear you and that you couldn't touch anything but doors. Does that sound like invisibility to you?"

Sam made a good point. "What could it be, then?"

She shrugged. "I don't know. It can't be a coincidence that you can only see Orson Wellington or the monster while you're invisible, but we can attack that problem later. You said you haven't spoken to Orson since Friday?"

I nodded.

"Then the first thing we should do is find him. He could be hurt and need our help. He might also be able to answer some of our questions."

"'We'?"

"No offense, Hector, but I'm pretty sure you need me."

In a way, Sam reminded me of Blake. Not the Blake who called me names, but the Blake who proposed wild ideas and was always confident we could pull them off. He never doubted himself, and he never doubted me, either. Sam radiated that same energy. With everything and everyone else seemingly out to get me, Sam felt safe.

"You're not going to tell Mr. Morhill, are you? I mean, he already knows about the ghost, but I'm not ready for anyone else to know I can turn invisible."

"Uncle Archie's pretty open-minded for an adult," Sam said. "But I won't mention anything you don't want me to."

"Thanks." Having Sam on my side, someone I could confide in again, made me feel less alone. "So what should we do first?"

Sam tapped her pen on her list. "Find Orson Wellington."

But to do that, I'd have to turn invisible and risk running into the monster again. "Now?"

"Sure. Why not?"

"What if I can't find him? What if the monster finds *me* instead? The monster could eat me, and there'd be no one around to tell my parents what happened." I shook my head.

"It's okay," Sam said. "I'll come up with a plan."

I felt so guilty. Orson had risked his life to save mine, but I was too afraid of the monster to go after him by myself.

Sam laid her hand on my arm. "Hey. We're in this together. You don't have to be scared anymore."

But I was, and she should have been too.

# 18

I WOKE UP Tuesday morning exhausted. I was sitting at the kitchen counter shoveling cereal into my mouth when Jason stumbled in, bleary-eyed. Pop took one look at him and scowled.

"Did you stay up late playing video games after I told you to go to bed?" Pop asked.

Jason shook his head and pointed at me. "He was crying and shouting in his sleep. Mumbling about someone named Orson."

I froze. I'd had nightmares about the tentacle. Sometimes it squeezed me like a boa constrictor; sometimes it ate me slowly. In one nightmare, it chased me around the school, but no matter where I went, I ran into more of its tentacles. Orson was in a lot of the nightmares, screaming for me to run or to help him or begging me not to leave him behind.

"Were you having bad dreams, Hector?" Mom asked.

"I guess," I said. "I don't remember."

"Who's Orson?" Pop said.

Jason snorted. "Probably his boyfriend."

"No he's not," I mumbled. "I don't know who he is."

"And," my mom said in a sharp tone directed at Jason, "even though I think Hector's a little young to be dating, if this Orson *were* his boyfriend, it wouldn't be something to tease him about."

Pop was conspicuously quiet, but Jason hung his head as he poured himself a bowl of cereal. He glared at me when I got up to go brush my teeth, and I feared the worst.

When Pop dropped us off at school, I headed for the library. Instead of going to play basketball, Jason jogged after me.

"Conrad Eldridge is telling everyone you asked Blake to be your boyfriend," Jason said, "and that's why you were fighting."

"So?"

"Is it true?"

I didn't know how to answer. I didn't want to say Conrad was lying when he wasn't, but the way Jason had joked about Orson being my boyfriend earlier made me worry about what he'd do if I answered honestly.

"Hey! Hector! Hurry up!" Sam stood at the steps to the library waving her arms. I was relieved to see her.

"Gotta go." I took off, leaving Jason behind, and followed Sam into the safety and cool air of the library.

"You okay?" she asked. "You look like you swallowed a bee."

Between the nightmares and finding out Conrad was telling everyone about me and Blake, I was out of sorts, but those weren't the most pressing problems. "I'm fine. So what's up? Do you have a plan for finding Orson?"

Sam's eyes seemed to glow. Her excitement was infectious. "Okay, we know that to find Orson you'll have to be invisible."

"But the monster—"

"Right," Sam said. "What if you take me with you?"

I frowned. "How?"

Sam waved her hands around as she talked. "I watched some movies last night for research. *The Invisible Man, Fantastic Four*—"

"*Fantastic Four* is research?"

"Duh," she said. "Anyway, in all the movies, people who turn invisible wind up naked. Why? Science stuff. I don't know. Point is, when you turned invisible, you weren't naked."

"Thankfully," I muttered.

"That means that maybe if you're holding on to something when you become invisible, like your clothes, it'll be invisible too!"

Sam's theory made sense. It wasn't like I'd had time to experiment with my ability before the monster scared me out of using it. Without waiting, I grabbed my backpack and made myself invisible. I counted to ten before turning back.

"Well? Did my bag change with me?"

Sam's smile was the only answer I needed. "Now me."

I took Sam's hand and willed us to become invisible. As soon as I began to change, I felt her fingers slip through mine.

"Why didn't that work?" Sam asked when I was visible again.

"Don't know."

Sam paced in front of the bookshelves. "So you can take objects with you, but not people. That's odd, but at least we know more than we did before."

"I want to find Orson and help him, but what if the monster's waiting for me? I can't face it alone." The sick, heavy feeling in my stomach returned. My body felt hot and prickly just thinking about the tentacle's teeth piercing my skin.

"You won't be alone. I was concerned my first plan wouldn't work, so I prepared a backup." Sam dug two compact walkie-talkies out of her bag. They looked expensive, not like the toy ones I had at home.

"What are those for?"

Sam handed me one. "Another test. I can't hear you while you're invisible, but maybe we can still talk through these."

Skeptical they would work, I turned on the walkie-talkie, and we tested them to make sure they were on the same frequency before I became invisible. The first thing I did was make sure the monster wasn't lurking around somewhere, but I didn't see it or Orson. When I was sure it was safe, I pressed the talk button. "Sam? Can you hear me?"

Sam smiled with her whole face. "I can hear you!" She

didn't even need to use the walkie because I could hear her without it.

"Hold up two fingers."

Sam held two fingers in the air. I became visible again, and she threw her arms around me. "It worked! With these, you can look for Orson, and we'll be able to stay in contact."

"You won't be able to help if I run into the monster, though."

Sam's enthusiasm wilted. "No, but this is the best we can do for now."

Orson could have left me behind in the hallway, but he hadn't. I had to try to help him. And since I'd be able to talk to Sam, I wouldn't be *totally* alone. "Okay. Let's do it. Do we have time now?"

Sam checked her watch and shook her head. "Today, though. I'll work something out even if I have to pull the fire alarm."

I hoped it wouldn't come to that. Fire drills were the worst.

During lunch detention, Miss DeVore led me across the hall to a locked room filled with filing cabinets and pointed at a stack of manila folders balanced on a chair. "Today, you'll be returning those to their proper places. The files are organized alphabetically by last name."

The room smelled musty and old, like my grandparents' house. "You don't have these on the computer?"

"I've been agitating to digitize them for years, but William is set in his ways."

I assumed she meant Principal O'Shea; I'd never heard anyone call him by his first name. "So I just stuff them in the right drawer?"

"Correct," Miss DeVore said. "I'll be across the hall. Shout if you need me."

Each time I opened a cabinet drawer, I released a cloud of dust into the air that tickled my nose and made me sneeze. It was slow, boring work. There were thousands of student records in the filing cabinets, going all the way back to when the school opened in 1955. As I was filing Chase Frick's record, I had an idea.

Miss DeVore said Coach Barbary had been a student at St. Lawrence's, so I dug around in the Bs until I found his file. Ulysses Eugene Barbary had been an honor student. He'd enrolled at St. Lawrence's in second grade and had graduated at the end of eighth grade. There was a school picture attached to the file. The boy peering back at me didn't look anything like the man who yelled at us to toughen up when we got hurt on the PE field. The boy in the photo wore heavy black-framed glasses and an apologetic smile. He was skinny, with huge ears, and his hair stuck up like a palm tree.

It was weird to think that Coach Barbary had ever been my age. Sometimes it felt like Mom and Pop and my teachers had been born adults. I wondered what I would turn into when I got old, and if I had any choice about growing up. Being an adult seemed like more trouble than it was worth.

After returning Coach Barbary's file, I dashed to the other end of the filing cabinets and pawed through the *W*s. I held my breath as I searched. Wakeley, Walford, Waller, Wasp, Watkins, Welbey. There it was! Wellington! I yanked out the file so quickly that the insides spilled onto the floor. I scrambled to gather them so Miss DeVore wouldn't find out.

Orson Wellington had been a student at St. Lawrence's from kindergarten until the middle of seventh grade, when his file simply ended. His teachers had written nice things about him. He'd been student of the month six times, and he'd even been an altar boy. He'd received grades for the first and second quarters of seventh grade, but nothing past that. In other students' files, it was noted if they'd transferred to a different school. But there was nothing indicating why Orson had left.

I wondered what would happen if I showed Miss DeVore Orson's file. Would she remember him? I suspected it would be like when I showed Orson's yearbook picture to Colonel Musser and the other teachers—she wouldn't be able to see it. The file didn't prove anything, except it made me suspect that Orson wasn't a ghost after all. Instead, it was like Orson Wellington had disappeared and the entire school had forgotten him. As I returned Orson's file to the cabinet, I couldn't help wondering: If I kept turning invisible, would the same thing happen to me?

# 19

I WAS BEGINNING to worry that Sam had forgotten about Orson, but then during my last period on Tuesday, she popped into my class and handed Mr. Grady a note. He read it and looked up, zeroing in on me. "Hector? Mr. Morhill has requested your help in the library for the remainder of class."

I packed up my books, stowed them in my cubby, and took my bag before following Sam into the hall. The second the door shut behind us, Sam grabbed my wrist and pulled me into the restroom.

"You got your walkie-talkie?" she asked.

"Yeah, but—" It dawned on me that we weren't going to the library.

Sam already had hers out, and she'd plugged an earpiece into it. "I'm going to hide here while you look for Orson. Talk to me, and it will be like I'm right beside you."

"Does Mr. Morhill know you sprang me from class?"

Sam waffled. "Kind of. Not really. But he'll cover for me. Don't worry about it."

"But—"

"We only have forty minutes, Hector."

As scared as I was, Sam was right, so I turned on my walkie and became invisible. "Can you hear me?"

Sam smiled. "I'll never get tired of seeing you do that." I waited for her to lock herself in the stall before leaving the restroom.

"Okay," I said. "I'm in the hallway. It's empty." The spot on my ankle where the monster had bitten me throbbed. I lifted my sock, expecting to find a bloody wound. Instead, the skin was a dark, splotchy purple. Kind of like the time Jason had stuck the vacuum cleaner against my leg and left a red hickey on my skin for a week.

"Check the classrooms before you go downstairs." It was weird hearing Sam's voice from the walkie-talkie, but I was grateful to have her with me. I peeked into each room as I passed. I spotted Blake looking out the window in Musser's class, and I watched Conrad Eldridge sleeping through religion, but Orson was nowhere to be seen. The closer I got to the stairwell, the harder it was to breathe. I had to force myself to keep moving forward.

"Nothing here. Going downstairs."

Sam must have heard the hitch in my voice, because she said, "You can do this, Hector."

I stuck my head into the stairwell, expecting to see Orson

or a slimy, toothy tentacle, but it was empty. I tiptoed all the way in and peered over the railing. Still nothing. I raced to the bottom as fast as I could, nearly tumbling down the last couple of steps, and reached the ground floor safely.

"Hector? Hector, talk to me."

"He's not in the stairwell," I said, breathlessly. "And no sign of the monster."

I checked the entire first floor before going outside. Orson wasn't in the parking lot, on the PE field, or in the library either.

"We've only got twenty minutes left," Sam said.

If I were a ghost, scared of a monster, where would I go? *I* probably would have gone to the library. I needed to know where Orson would have gone, which was difficult since I didn't know him at all. I looked around, stopping when my eyes landed on St. Lawrence's church. Orson's file said he'd been an altar boy! I raced across the lot and slipped through the heavy church doors. There were a few people kneeling in front of the prayer candles, and Father Allison was sitting by the confessionals talking quietly to an elderly man. I thought I might've gotten it wrong and was about to leave when I spotted Orson's head among the pews in the far corner.

"Orson Wellington!"

Orson turned around, and I don't think I've ever seen anyone so happy to see me in my whole life. "Hector!" He leapt up, raced across the church, and nearly knocked me over with a hug. "I thought you'd forgotten about me!"

"You're okay?" I didn't know Orson well enough to be comfortable with him hugging me, but I also figured I might have been the first real person he'd been around in years. "I was worried the monster had gotten you. What was that thing? Why are you here? What happened to you?"

I must've been silent on the walkie-talkie too long because Sam was trying to get my attention. "Hector? Hector, what's going on? We've got ten minutes until the bell rings. Hector?"

Orson finally let me go. He knuckled the tears from his eyes and motioned at the walkie. "Who's that?"

I pressed the button to talk to Sam. "I'm okay. I found him. Sam, this is Orson, Orson, this is Sam. She's hiding in the restroom."

Orson eyed the walkie suspiciously. "The restroom? *She?* Are they letting girls into St. Lawrence's now? Because I always thought they should."

Sam was trying to talk to me, but I asked her to hold on a minute so I could listen to Orson. "Are you hurt?"

Orson shook his head. "I've gotten good at hiding from the gelim."

"Gelim?"

"The monster," he said.

"I have so many questions, but school's about to let out." If I was late meeting Pop, I'd be in more trouble than I already was. "Can you come to the library tomorrow morning before school?"

"Why?" Orson asked.

"So Sam and I can try to help you, obviously."

Orson leaned against a pew and bowed his head. "You can't help me. No one can."

I rested my hand on Orson's shoulder. "You don't know that. At least let us try."

Tears ran freely down Orson's cheeks this time. "It's been so long since I've talked to someone."

I felt awful for him. I didn't mind being alone to read or play piano, but I couldn't imagine spending three years by myself. I pressed the walkie-talkie into Orson's hand. "Keep this. You'll have a way to reach us when we're at school."

Orson nodded. "Okay, but—"

"I promise Sam and I will meet you tomorrow morning before school in the library." I wished I didn't have to go, but I was out of time. "Stay safe until then."

Orson hugged the walkie-talkie to his chest like it was a mint-condition *Batman* #3. "I'll try."

I ran back to the main building and hoped I'd see Orson tomorrow.

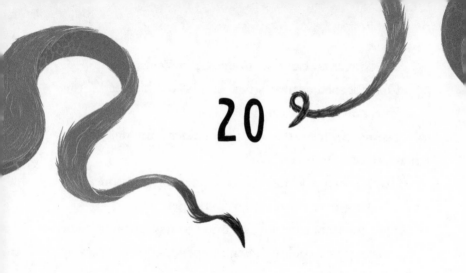

# 20

MR. MORHILL WAVED cheerfully at me when I arrived at the library Wednesday morning. I felt bad about Sam using her connection to him to sneak me out of class the day before. Between setting fire to Blake's project, keeping secrets from my mom, and skipping class, I was feeling guilty about a lot lately, and it was eating at me. Maybe Blake wasn't the only person who was changing.

Sam was waiting for me in the music room. As soon as I arrived, she shut the doors and locked them so we wouldn't be disturbed. She was pacing impatiently. "Orson?" she said into her walkie-talkie. "Orson? Are you there?"

"If he's in the room, he'll be able to hear you without the walkie," I said.

"However, if he's *not* here but is within range with the radio on, he'll hear me."

"Good point."

Unfortunately, Orson didn't answer. I prayed he was okay and that the monster hadn't gotten him.

Sam called him again.

Finally, Orson's voice came through the walkie. "I'm here."

I let go of the breath I'd been holding and became invisible so I could see Orson. He was sitting on a stool I would have sworn hadn't been there before, and he popped up when I appeared.

"Hector! I've been here all night so I wouldn't miss you. It's not safe to be in the school after dark, though. Usually I sleep in the church, but what if I overslept? I couldn't risk it. And then I was so nervous that I dropped the walkie-talkie, which is why it took so long for me to respond!" Words poured from Orson like water from a busted pipe. "How are you here? How do you travel back and forth? And how is there a girl at St. Lawrence's?"

"Guys?" Sam said. "You know I can't hear you if you don't use the walkie-talkie, right?"

I took the radio from Orson and pressed the button. "Sorry, Sam. We're here. Both of us. Orson is okay."

"Hi, Sam!" Orson said. "Nice to kind of meet you."

I had a ton of questions to ask Orson, but one fought to the front of the line. "Are we safe?"

Orson's energy shifted. His shoulders slumped and he drifted back to sit on the piano bench. I held the transmit button on the walkie so Sam could hear us.

"Safe-*ish*," Orson said. "The gelim's a little more sluggish during the day, but it doesn't really sleep. Neither do I. Not here. Nothing sleeps here."

There were no other chairs I could sit on, so I plopped down on the floor across from Orson. "It didn't seem sluggish when it was trying to eat me."

Orson's chin dipped to his chest. "That was my fault. I was poking around the old clergy house, trying to find a way in, and I must've alerted the gelim. I'm pretty sure that's where it nests."

"I knew that place was creepy!"

Orson looked up, caught my eye. "You have no idea, Hector. What you saw of the gelim isn't even a fraction of it."

"The one tentacle was bad enough." I didn't want to think about what the rest of the monster looked like or I might not sleep for the rest of my life. "If its nest is in the clergy house, why were you trying to get inside?"

"To find the gelim's weakness, if it has one," Orson said. "But the place is locked up tight."

"What's that you keep calling the monster?" Sam asked.

"Gelim," Orson said.

Sam frowned. "Sounds like golem."

"Do golems have tentacles?"

I'd read about golems, and I doubted anyone would have intentionally created the monster that had attacked me and Orson. "I don't think this is a golem, Sam."

"Gelim is just what it's called," Orson said. "I don't know

what it means. It's just written on a wall. I can show you sometime."

"Really?" I asked.

"We could go now."

Sam cleared her throat. "What happened to you?" she asked, sounding impatient. It must've been weird trying to have a conversation with two boys she couldn't see. "How did you get stuck invisible?"

"Invisible?"

I nodded. "Like me."

Orson chuckled. "I'm not invisible, and neither are you."

Under her breath, Sam said, "I had a feeling . . ."

But I was confused. "If I'm not invisible, then what am I?"

"Lost," Orson said. "You're where lost things go."

I opened my mouth to ask a question, but Sam beat me to it. "So you're not a ghost?"

"I sure hope not."

"This doesn't make sense," I said. "I'm not lost."

Orson bit his bottom lip. "That's just what *I* call it. It could be something else. All I know is I've been here a long time, and I've seen things. Stuff winds up here."

"Stuff?" I said.

Orson nodded. "You know how sometimes a thing disappears? And you know you had it, but no matter where you look, you can't find it?"

"Yeah," Sam and I answered in unison.

"Chances are, it winds up here."

"Like missing socks?" Sam said.

"Probably." Orson paused. "Toys people used to love. Gifts they didn't really want. Belongings they were careless with. It all winds up here, lost and forgotten."

Sam had gotten out her notebook and was writing everything down. "So you're not invisible—you're in an actual different place? That's why no one can see you or hear you?"

"But I heard you," I said. "By the clergy house and in the stairwell."

Orson bit his thumbnail. "You heard me in the stairwell because you were here in the lost place, just like now, but that was the first time I ever spoke to you."

I shook my head. "That can't be right. It was last week. I was running from Blake and you called my name from the clergy house."

Orson's face grew grave. "That wasn't me. If I had to guess, I'd say it was the gelim trying to lure you inside."

A shiver ran through me. The monster, the gelim, had been calling me that day, and I'd nearly fallen into its trap.

Orson stood and paced around the room. He was like a swarm of hornets trapped in the shape of a boy. "I don't know why you would have heard it, though. You shouldn't be able to hear the gelim unless you're here."

"Orson?" Sam said. "Why have you been in that place so long? Why don't you return the way Hector does?"

"Don't you think I would if I could?" Orson snapped. "It's not like I haven't spent every day trying."

"What about—" I began, but Sam interrupted me.

"School's starting soon," she said. "Hector, you should try to bring Orson back with you."

That hadn't occurred to me, especially after failing to make Sam invisible. "Do you think I can?"

"Do you?" Orson added, his annoyance veering sharply toward hope.

Sam looked up from the notebook she was writing in. "We won't know until we try."

I glanced at Orson and held out my hand. He was trembling, but he pressed his palm to mine and we laced our fingers together.

"Here goes nothing." I willed myself to become visible, but Orson felt like an anchor tied to my ankle, preventing me from moving.

"I knew it wouldn't work," Orson said, sounding defeated.

"Let me try again," I said.

This time I shut my eyes and focused entirely on making Orson and myself visible. I tuned out the thousand questions I wanted to ask, my wonder at finding myself in an entirely different world, and my fear of the gelim. For a few seconds, Orson was my entire universe. Nothing mattered but bringing him home.

"I see you!" Sam said.

Even with my eyes closed, I could feel something happening, but suddenly I snapped back like I was tethered to a pole and I'd reached the end of my leash.

I tried again, straining until spots danced in my vision and my skin prickled with sweat, but we remained invisible. When I opened my eyes and saw Orson's defeated look, I felt like the monster for giving him hope and then snatching it away.

"Hector? Are you there?"

I pressed the button on the walkie. "I'm here, Sam. It didn't work."

"The bell's going to ring any minute," she said. "Come back and we'll figure out another way to rescue Orson."

Orson reluctantly let go of my hand. "It's okay."

"Wait right there," I said, and turned visible. Sam heaved a sigh of relief when she saw me.

"Don't worry, Orson," Sam said. "I know there's a way to save you, and we *will* find it."

Sam's walkie-talkie crackled before Orson's voice came through. "Don't. And don't come here again either. The only thing worse than being alone would be if you got lost permanently because you were trying to help me."

"Orson? Wait!"

The door opened and shut. Orson was gone.

# 21

COACH BARBARY DIDN'T care that I could turn invisible or that a student had been lost in some strange place for three years, or that there was a monster roaming school grounds. He didn't *know* any of those things, but if he had, he still wouldn't have cared. The only thing that made him smile was causing his students to suffer. I'd hoped that after a few days of making us run, he'd forget about our punishment and let me and Blake rejoin the others, but at the beginning of each PE class, Coach asked us if we were ready to tell him why we were fighting, and each time we didn't answer, he told us to run. It wasn't fair.

"Seen any monsters lately?" Blake said with a sneer as we jogged.

"Not today," I said. "But it's real, and you know it." Sometimes Blake took off on his own; other times he jogged alongside me. I suspected he was looking for an opportunity to call me names or do something awful, but I couldn't help hoping he was trying to find a way to apologize.

"Sure, *freak*."

"Maybe *you're* the monster," I muttered.

"Maybe I am."

I glanced at Blake. It was like someone had sucked the color out of him and turned him into a bland, gray husk. With each day that passed, Blake seemed even less like the person I used to confide my secrets in. Eventually, there'd be nothing left of him that I'd recognize. When that day came, my best friend would be gone for good.

As we neared the clergy house, I heard a wet grinding noise, like a bone stuck in the garbage disposal, followed by a cry for help. I slowed and stopped, kneeling to pretend to tie my shoe. Blake kept jogging. He didn't even look back. When he was far enough away, I called Orson's name.

The sound was coming from inside the old clergy house. Orson had said it was where the gelim made its nest. My instincts told me to steer clear of the clergy house, but my conscience wouldn't let me walk away if there was a chance Orson or someone else needed help. I stayed visible as I crept around the side of the building. I stood on a pipe coming out of the side of the house and tried to peek through the shuttered window, but the glass was so thick with dust that I couldn't see anything within.

"Orson?"

My skin felt like it was trying to crawl off my bones and run in the opposite direction. This was a bad idea. Maybe

I'd only imagined hearing someone because I felt guilty for not being able to rescue Orson.

When I reached the door, the first thing I noticed was that the dead bolt was drawn. The house was practically inviting me inside. All I had to do was enter, poke around, make sure Orson wasn't in trouble, and get out again. I probably wouldn't even see the gelim. Anyway, I bet Orson had exaggerated how terrible it was. He'd probably injured it when he'd stabbed it with those scissors. It was probably weak and hurting. I'd just pop in and check and then be on my way.

"Hector Griggs? You better have a good explanation for why you're not running." Coach Barbary's voice hit me like a bucket of ice water.

I shook my head. What had I been about to do? My hand was on the knob. Another couple of seconds and I would have gone inside. I stumbled away from the door. "I don't . . . I thought I heard something."

Coach Barbary gripped my shoulder and half pushed, half dragged me back to the school. I hadn't even noticed that class was over. The other boys were already in the locker room changing. When we reached Coach's office, he shut the door and pointed to a seat.

I still felt dazed and weak. I couldn't believe I'd almost gone into the clergy house, even after Orson had told me it was dangerous. Coach pushed a bottle of Gatorade into my hand.

"Drink it."

I twisted off the cap and gulped it down.

Coach was sitting on the corner of his desk with his arms folded over his chest, looking at me with a frown that etched deep lines around his eyes and across his forehead. "What were you doing by the clergy house, Hector? It's off-limits to students."

The Gatorade was helping—I felt more clearheaded—but I didn't know what to tell Coach. How was I supposed to explain that a monster he couldn't see had nearly tricked me into walking into its trap? "Um . . . I thought I heard someone."

"Someone?" Coach asked. "Or some*thing?* Earlier you said *something.*"

I shrugged and looked down at my shoes, but I could still feel Coach staring at me.

Finally he said, "Go get changed."

"Yes, sir." I stood.

"But if I see you near the clergy house again, you're going to be running laps until you graduate eighth grade. Do you understand me?"

"Yes, sir."

- - - - - -

Miss DeVore stuck me in the file room again for lunch. As soon as she was gone, I called Orson on the walkie-talkie. I wasn't sure he would answer or if he was even listening. "Hey, I know you're probably disappointed about what happened earlier, but I'm not going to give up. It'll be easier if you talk to me so that I can learn more about the lost place and the gremlin or whatever you called the monster, but I'm going to keep trying to help you either way."

I held the walkie-talkie to my ear. Nothing. I pressed the button to talk again. "Come on, Orson. Please say something. Anything."

"You're very persistent." Orson's voice came through the walkie loud and clear.

I was so happy to hear him that I nearly dropped the radio. "Where are you?"

"Here," Orson said. "In the file room."

"How'd you get in? I didn't see the door open."

"Followed you in."

I turned invisible and found Orson sitting on top of the filing cabinets. "You've been here the whole time?"

"Yeah. Sorry for storming off before."

"I get it." In Orson's place, I probably would have run off too. I pointed at the walkie-talkie. "You should turn that off to conserve the battery."

Orson shook his head. "Don't need to. Batteries don't die here."

"Really? That's kind of amazing."

"There's nothing to eat, and I won't die of hunger, but I'm always hungry. I can't sleep, but I'm always tired. I'm still the same age I was three years ago when I got stuck here." Orson chuckled ruefully. "So, yeah, really amazing except for all the ways it sucks."

I held up a finger. "Don't go anywhere." Before Orson

could respond, I became visible, grabbed my backpack where I'd dropped it on the floor, and shifted again. I reached into my bag, pulled out my lunch sack, and tossed it to Orson. He peered inside and stared. Tears welled in his eyes and rolled down his cheeks.

Orson dug into the bag for the peanut butter and jelly sandwich my mom had packed me, unwrapped it, and took a huge bite. "I hate PB and J so much. Thank you." After the initial bite, he ate slower, savoring every crumb.

I gave Orson a minute to enjoy his first meal in three years. Then I asked, "Were you by the clergy house today? I swear I heard you call for help."

Orson shook his head. "I told you it's the gelim. It messes with you. Makes you hear things. Lures you in."

And I'd nearly fallen for it again.

I didn't want to bombard Orson with questions, but I had a ton, so I figured I'd start with an easy one. "How'd you get stuck like this?"

Orson brushed bread crumbs off his uniform before pulling out the bag of Cheetos. He opened the bag and stuck his nose in, inhaling deeply.

"Do you hate Cheetos too?" I asked.

"They're my favorite." Orson held one between his fingers and ate it like it was the last Cheeto in existence. I guess I would've been a little weird about food if I hadn't eaten anything in three years.

"You ever notice how white this school is?" Orson said. "I was the only Black kid here until I was in fifth grade, and then the other one was a first grader, so it's not like we were gonna hang out."

Orson was right. Jackson was *still* the only Black student at the school. And, not including him, there were only seven other non-white students. Eight total out of five hundred. "That must've been lonely."

"Yeah," Orson said. "I was always looking for places where I could hide and read. I was good at it too. So good that one day I must've slipped through a crack and wound up here. I thought it was the coolest thing at first. I'd found this whole other world! Then I realized I couldn't get back. I kept looking for a way out, but days passed with no luck. I thought maybe going home would help, but my parents had forgotten me. The house was filled with evidence of my life, but my parents couldn't see it. As far as they were concerned, they'd never had a son."

"I'm so sorry." I tried to imagine if Mom and Pop forgot I existed, and it made me feel like my stomach was full of thorns.

"It wasn't long after that the gelim started hunting me."

"Do you know *why* you got stuck?" I asked.

Orson shook his head. He'd finished the Cheetos and pulled the bag apart so he could lick the dust from the inside. "Don't know why you're able to come and go freely, either, but you should stop before you get trapped too."

"You can't expect me to leave you behind and forget about you."

Orson mumbled, "Everyone else did."

"Please let me help you," I said. "Meet me here again tomorrow. Teach me what you know about this place, and maybe together we can find a solution to get you home." I didn't blame Orson for being cautious. I'd already gotten his hopes up once.

Orson looked up and caught my eye. "Can you bring me something else to eat?"

"Anything."

"Anything but PB and J?"

I grinned. "Deal."

# 22

MOM STOOD WITH her hands on her hips, frowning. "Why do you have two sandwiches, Hector?"

The whole thing started Thursday morning because Lee saw me trying to pack an extra bag of chips, and he complained that when *he'd* tried to take extra chips, he'd gotten yelled at. That led to Mom emptying my lunch sack and finding out that I'd packed two lunches. I couldn't tell her that one was for a boy who was trapped in some kind of weird pocket dimension where monsters were real and batteries lived forever.

"Because I'm hungry."

"Yeah," Lee said. "Me too." He tried to grab a second pack of Nutty Buddy bars, but Pop smacked his hand.

"Are you sure this food is for you?" Mom asked. "A bully isn't forcing you to give them your lunch, are they?"

"No one's making me give them my lunch." At least that part was true. I hated lying to my mom so much.

"The boy *could* stand to put on some weight," Pop said.

Mom sighed. "You can have a second sandwich, but not chips or Nutty Buddy bars. I'm not going to have you filling up on junk."

It wasn't a total win, but I didn't mind giving up my chips and dessert to Orson as long as I didn't have to go totally hungry—by the time I'd gotten home from school the day before, I'd been starving.

Sam was waiting for me outside the library when Pop dropped me and Jason off at school. She was playing a game on her Switch and didn't look up when I sat beside her until she reached a save point. I hadn't told her about what had happened the day before at lunch, so I filled her in while she played.

"I don't think you should turn invisible again until we know more about what's going on and where you're going." Sam put her Switch in the front pocket of her backpack and zipped it shut.

"But I promised Orson."

"The gelim's tried to lure you into the clergy house twice now. It's dangerous, Hector. Besides, you could get stuck there like Orson."

"So we're going to quit? We promised Orson we'd help him."

Sam rested her hand on my arm. "And we will. But first we need more information."

"About?"

"Everything," Sam said. "What's happening to you when you become invisible or go where the lost things wind up or whatever you want to call it. We need more information about the gelim. Can it be hurt? What does it want with you and Orson? Does it have anything to do with your friend Blake and the boys he's hanging out with?"

"How are we going to learn any of that stuff without talking to Orson?"

"That's what the walkie-talkies are for," Sam said.

It seemed like Sam had an answer for everything. And it wasn't like she was wrong: the smart thing to do would have been to investigate slowly so no one got hurt. But Orson was stuck on the other side with a monster. Our caution could cost him his life. "There has to be something we can do."

Sam sighed. "I'm working on it, Hector. Just promise me you won't turn invisible until we know more."

"I can't," I said. "I made a promise to Orson first."

"Then can you at least promise you'll be careful?"

I smiled. "That I can do."

- - - - - -

Miss DeVore was busy dealing with the parents of a potential new student and didn't have time for me. She sent me to the file room to continue organizing the records. Even if I'd had detention for a year, I couldn't have finished. Orson was waiting for me, and he beamed when I appeared holding the lunch I'd promised.

"I hope tuna's okay."

Orson tore into the sandwich. "So good."

I figured we were going to hang out in the file room and eat, but Orson motioned for me to follow him.

"C'mon. Something I want to show you."

I wasn't sure leaving was a good idea, but I had a feeling Miss DeVore was going to be too preoccupied to check up on me. "Aren't you worried about the monster?"

Orson shook his head as he worked on the sandwich. "When it's close, I feel this itch on the soles of my feet, but they're itch-free today." He opened the door to the hall and left. I followed, shutting the door behind me.

"What's the deal with doors?" I asked. "How come I can touch those but not much else?"

"You want to prank someone? Knock over their drink or make something float and scare them?" Orson chuckled. "I tried it too. But objects don't really have a presence here unless they're lost or permanent."

"Permanent?"

"Yeah," Orson said. "The building's not gonna up and walk away, but desks get shuffled around a lot, which is why you can't move them. The longer an object sits in one place, the more tangible it becomes. As long as an object stays rooted, you can touch it on this side."

"But doors change. They open and close all the time."

"Doors are special. I think doors exist everywhere."

Orson led me across the lot to the church, and inside, behind the altar to a storage room with chairs and boxes stacked neatly along the walls. In the corner was a nest of sweatshirts and blankets, and there were objects everywhere. Scissors, pencil cases, sneakers, keys, books.

"This is my safe room," Orson said.

"What is all this junk?"

"Lost stuff that's slipped through the cracks from your world to this one. All the belongings people lose or forget about eventually wind up here." Orson sat on the blankets on the floor to finish his lunch. "When it's safe, I go out scavenging." He dug around his stash until he found a silver bangle set with a turquoise stone. "Colonel Musser lost this last year."

He tossed it to me, and I caught it. Inside was engraved J. M. MUSSER. It must've been important to her. I wondered how she'd lost it.

"I've also got two sets of Mrs. Ford's keys," Orson said, "and Coach Barbary's glasses."

"Coach doesn't wear glasses."

"Not when students are around."

"What do you do with all this stuff?" I asked, looking around at the random collection of belongings.

Orson shrugged. "Nothing. Some of it was here before I arrived, and hunting for lost things gives me something to do."

"There was already stuff here?" I said. "Does that mean there are other people trapped in this place?"

"I think there were," Orson said. "But I've never seen them." He leaned to the side and pointed at the wall behind him. "That's where I got the monster's name."

Etched into the wood by something sharp was a poem:

GONE TOMORROW,
LOST TODAY,
THE GELIM IS THE HUNTER,
WE ARE THE PREY.
GONE FOREVER,
FORGOTTEN FOR GOOD,
THE GELIM IS COMING,
I MISS MY MOM.

I stared at the words, feeling the fear of the person who'd carved them one line at a time into the wood wall. I hoped they'd escaped, but something told me they hadn't. "Can anyone on the other side see this?" I pointed at the poem.

"No." Orson frowned. "Doors are the only thing we have any effect on while we're here. You could bulldoze the church on this side, and it would remain standing over there."

"Oh." I was still holding Musser's bangle, turning it over in my hands. There was something odd about it that tickled my brain. "How do you know if something is lost?"

"Aside from being able to pick it up?" Orson said. "Lost stuff doesn't have a shadow."

"Seriously?"

Orson stood. "Come on. It's easier to show you outside."

I set the bangle down and followed. When we reached the parking lot, Orson pointed at the asphalt. "See? Lost things don't cast a shadow here."

Even standing under the bright sun, I didn't have a shadow, and neither did Orson. I spun around a couple times and hopped up and down, but it was like the sun's rays were passing through me. That was what had been bothering me about the bangle! I couldn't believe I hadn't noticed it sooner. When the novelty of not having a shadow wore off, I said, "I should get back in case Miss DeVore checks on me."

While we walked to the file room, I said, "Why do you think you're stuck here?"

Orson shoved his hands in his pockets. "Probably the gelim. I think it's like a spider and this whole place is its web."

"Does that make us the flies?"

Orson nodded. "It lures us here, traps us, and then the world forgets we existed."

"But you've been here three years. Why has it waited so long to . . ."

"Eat me?" Orson said. "I have a theory that the gelim feeds on fear, so I guess you could say it *has* been feeding on me this whole time."

I shivered. *The gelim is the hunter, we are the prey.* "How do we stop it?"

"We can't."

"But you hurt it when you stabbed it in the hallway."

"I only irritated it," Orson said. I tried to argue again, but he held up his hand to cut me off. "If every student at this school attacked the gelim at once, we *might* be able to overwhelm it, but alone?" He shook his head grimly. "Since I can't leave like you can, the best I can do is hide and hope it never finds me."

Nothing had been disturbed in the file room, which I hoped meant Miss DeVore hadn't checked on me and realized I was gone. "Tomorrow's my last day of detention, so we'll have to figure out a different time to meet up."

"Why not lunch?"

"If I'm missing from the cafeteria too often, someone might notice, but don't worry. I'm not going to forget about you."

Orson nodded. "Thank you, Hector."

"For what?"

"The sandwiches. Talking to me." Orson's shoulders fell. "You don't know what it's like to go years without hearing your name. Sometimes it got so bad, I even thought about letting the gelim find me just so I'd know I was still real."

I had no idea how lonely Orson had really been. I hated having to leave him, but the bell rang, ending lunch, and I couldn't be late to class. "I'll see you—"

"Promise me you'll come back," Orson said. It sounded like a command and a desperate plea at the same time.

"Of course I will."

"But say it, okay? Promise you won't leave me. That you won't forget me." Orson's voice was soft, pleading.

I couldn't have refused if I'd wanted to. "I swear it."

Orson's entire mood changed as he busted out a toothy grin. "You're the best! I'm going to figure out a way to pay you back for everything you've done."

"You don't have to."

"I know," Orson said, "but I want to. I owe you so much. Just trust me, all right? It's going to be great!"

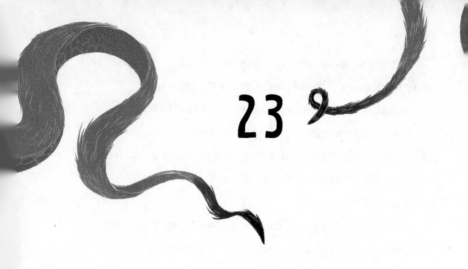

# 23

BLAKE WAS IN a good mood Friday, which made me
nervous. He'd been smiling while he changed into his gym
clothes and was already running laps by the time Coach
Barbary reached the field. I hadn't seen him this happy since
his birthday over the summer when his parents bought him
a surfboard. I figured the best thing I could do was avoid
him, but Blake had other plans.

"I don't know why we were ever friends," Blake said.
"You're not funny; you're not good at sports. All you do is
whine and play piano."

I tried not to let him hurt me, but every word landed
like a punch. "Stop it. Please?"

"No."

"Blake—"

"One day your new friend and those cupcakes you sit

with are going to see the truth about you," Blake said. "And then you won't have anyone."

I wanted to tell Blake he was wrong, but there was a time not so long ago when I would've said Blake would never do anything to hurt me and that we would be best friends forever, so maybe he was right. Maybe the guys at lunch would get sick of me, and Sam would decide I had too many problems and wasn't worth the trouble. Even Orson would probably be better off if he found someone else to help him, because the chances of me succeeding were slim.

I had to get away from Blake. I slowed to let him pass me, but he matched my speed. I ran faster; he sped up. Blake didn't talk the rest of PE, but he paced me the entire time, taunting me with his smile.

When the bell rang, I took off for the locker room, happy I wouldn't have to spend another second near Blake. But when I got to my locker, it was standing wide open, and it was empty.

"Who took my stuff?" The other boys were trickling in, and I looked to them for answers. "Luke? Arjun?" They pretended they couldn't hear me. I caught Gordi's eye. "C'mon, Gordi. Where are my backpack and clothes?"

Gordi started to answer, but then Blake walked in and Gordi's mouth snapped shut.

"Forget it. I'll find them myself." I stomped around the locker room until I heard laughter coming from the toilets. A couple of boys and Blake were hanging out by the stalls. Dread made a nest in my stomach as I moved closer to peer inside. My uniform had been stuffed into one toilet, and everything in my backpack had been emptied into another.

Every time I thought Blake couldn't sink lower, he proved that there were depths to his meanness I hadn't known existed. I couldn't believe he was the same person who'd stood up for me at the beach last summer when some older boys had tried to steal my bike even though they were bigger and outnumbered us. *That* Blake never would've trashed my stuff and laughed about it, but that Blake was gone, and I didn't know *what* had replaced him.

Coach Barbary marched in, surveyed the scene, and then turned on the boys who'd gathered around to watch. "Who did this?"

"Don't look at me," Blake said. "I was running with Hector all period. Maybe it was the monster. Or was it a ghost? You did tell me you'd seen a ghost, right, Hector?"

A few of the boys snickered, but a single look from Coach silenced them.

"Salvage what you can, Hector," Coach said. "You can wear your PE clothes the rest of the day."

"Yes, sir." My voice was barely a whimper.

"As for the rest of you, you can *all* run laps next week."

Groans echoed through the locker room. Maybe Coach thought he was helping, but he'd only made things worse.

- - - - - -

"It was Conrad," I told Sam as we walked downstairs from our homerooms to go to lunch. "It had to be. Somehow he got out of class and trashed my stuff during PE."

Everything in my backpack had been ruined. My books, my homework, my lunch and Orson's. Even the walkie-talkie.

"Don't let them get you down," Sam said. "Tell Orson I'll get new walkie-talkies, and I'll work on a plan this weekend to help him."

When we reached the ground floor, Sam split off to go to the cafeteria while I headed to the principal's office for my last day of detention with Miss DeVore. We were stuffing envelopes again. I felt bad that Orson was probably waiting in the file room for me to bring him lunch and I couldn't get away to tell him why I wasn't coming. Not that I had anything to give him, because of Conrad. I hoped he'd peek out and see I was stuck in the office and wouldn't be mad if I wasn't able to hang out with him until Monday.

"You're unusually quiet today," Miss DeVore said. "And fragrant."

"Someone shoved my stuff in a toilet," I mumbled.

"How rude." Miss DeVore continued folding letters and handing them to me to stuff in envelopes. "Do you know who the culprit is?"

"I have an idea, but I can't prove it."

Miss DeVore *hmm*ed. "The names and faces of the boys at this school may change, but one thing that never does is that some boys are bullies and some are victims. I wouldn't have expected you to fall into the latter category."

"What do you mean?"

"A smart boy like you could surely find a way to send a message to your tormentors that you aren't to be trifled with."

I'd already tried revenge, but that hadn't worked out so well. "It doesn't matter."

"Of course it matters, Hector. Are you a man or a mouse?"

"Squeak?"

Miss DeVore laughed.

While we continued stuffing envelopes, I had an idea. My teachers hadn't remembered Orson, but maybe Miss DeVore would. "You've worked here a long time, right?"

Miss DeVore stared down her nose at me. "It's unkind to remind a lady that she's old. But, to answer your question, yes."

"Do you remember a student named Orson Wellington?"

"What an unusual name. He was a student here?"

I nodded.

"I'm not certain how I'd have forgotten such a distinctive name, but it doesn't sound familiar."

That figured. "What about the ghost? Do you know anything about it?"

Miss DeVore's pale eyes lit up. "Well now, you boys have been telling stories about St. Lawrence's being haunted for as long as I can remember. Children have passed through this office blaming the ghost for everything from missing homework to clogged toilets."

"Have *you* ever seen anything strange?"

"Like a ghost?" She paused, eyeing me with a hint of a smile. "Or a monster?" Miss DeVore shook her head. "No."

"Oh."

"But that doesn't mean they aren't real. Sometimes children, especially sensitive children, are capable of seeing and hearing things beyond the perception of adults."

Like how I'd heard the gelim even before I'd first turned invisible.

The bell rang.

"Well, Hector, as much as I've enjoyed your company this week, I hope I won't see you here again."

"Thank you, Miss DeVore."

"Now run along. And say hi to your ghost for me."

# 24

EITHER MOM HAD forgotten about my punishment or she'd run out of things for me to clean. I'd had nightmares about the gelim the night before, and all I wanted to do Saturday was sit in my room and read quietly, but Jason and Lee decided they were bored and wanted to play hunter, a game they'd made up. It was basically hide-and-seek mixed with tag, where the hunters—usually Jason and Lee—searched for the prey, usually me. They only won if they "killed" me. I hated the game, but Jason and Lee loved it. Especially the killing part. This time, however, I had an advantage, and they were surprised when I agreed to play.

As soon as the boys went to Lee's room so I could hide, I turned invisible. At first it was fun watching Jason and Lee run around looking for me, but I quickly got bored and decided to explore. I found countless lost socks, Jason's watch, two of Lee's retainers, and a card Grandma had given me for my tenth birthday with twenty dollars in it. I left the retainers but pocketed the money.

I wondered if the gelim at school was the only monster in the place where lost things wound up or if there were other, worse monsters lurking in the dark. Just thinking about that possibility made me want to turn visible again, but I remembered what Mom had told me when I was little and I was scared of spiders. She said that the best way to not be afraid of something was to understand it and took me to the library to find books about arachnids. I learned the names of different types of spiders, how they were responsible for eating bugs that got into the house, how some people even thought they were lucky. By the time I was done, I didn't like spiders any better, but I wasn't scared of them anymore either.

So maybe the key to beating the gelim was to understand it. I went to my room, quickly grabbed my tablet, and disappeared again. I searched for a monster named *gelim*. The first results were for a type of Persian rug, but that obviously wasn't right. The search engine suggested *golem* and *gremlin* as possibilities, but those weren't right either. I tried searching for monsters with tentacles, but there were way too many, so I narrowed it down to monsters that preyed on kids. In Japan, they had the aobōzu, a spirit that kidnapped children who stayed out late. There was Krampus, a demon who stuffed naughty kids in a sack and beat them during the Christmas season in Austria. In Serbia they had a bauk, which hid in dark places and dragged off its prey to devour it. Haiti had the Mètminwi, which ate anyone out late on the streets. There was Black Annis, a blue-faced witch who haunted the countryside of Leicestershire, England, and ate and wore the skins of any children she found. There was also Gurumāpā of Nepal, Il-Belliegħa of Malta, and Oude Rode Ogen of Belgium. Unfortunately, none of the monsters matched what I'd seen in the stairwell that day, and nothing I learned provided me clues for how to beat the gelim.

While researching, I must have dozed off, because the next thing I knew, Mom was calling my name and she sounded panicked. I turned visible and ran from my room to the kitchen.

As soon as Mom saw me, she hugged me so tight she was smothering me. Then she held me out by my shoulders and shook me. "Where have you been?"

"In my room," I said. "I must've fallen asleep."

"Don't you dare lie to me, Hector Myles Griggs!" My mom hardly ever used my middle name. "Roy is out looking for you. I called your piano teacher; I called Blake's house."

"I swear, I was in my bedroom. I was reading and—"

"Don't you think your room was the first place I checked?" Mom let go of me and called Pop to tell him she'd found me. When she was done, she looked at me from the bottom of a deep well of disappointment. "What is going on with you? Fighting? Lying? This isn't like you at all."

"I'm not the one who's different!" I said. "Before you married Pop, you would've believed me!"

Mom's eyes softened. "This isn't about Pop or the boys—"

"Why not? Everything else is."

I knew right away that I'd crossed the line. Mom's mouth tightened and her nostrils flared. "Go to your room," she said. "And don't even think about coming out until you're ready to start telling the truth."

"Yes, ma'am." I trudged to my room, buried my face in my pillow, and cried.

# 25

**MOM BARELY TALKED** to me the rest of the weekend. She'd been angry at me before, but never like this. It was so bad that even Jason and Lee didn't pick on me as much as they normally did. I was actually grateful when Monday came around and I had to go to school.

I went straight to the library after Pop dropped me and Jason off, and I found Sam waiting for me in the music room. "I need to check on Orson," I said, and then turned invisible without waiting for her to respond.

Orson was standing by the door, and he looked so happy to see me that it hurt.

"I'm sorry I didn't get to visit you Friday afternoon. Miss DeVore had me stuffing envelopes."

"I know," Orson said. "It's okay. I also saw what happened to your stuff in PE. It was that eighth-grade boy your ex–best friend's always hanging around with."

"Conrad?" I said. "I knew it!"

Sam cleared her throat. "Uh, Hector? Orson?"

"Hold tight," I said to Orson, and then turned visible again. "I was right. It was Conrad Eldridge who ruined my stuff Friday."

Sam handed me a new walkie-talkie. "I set this one to the same frequency as the other."

I clicked the walkie on. "Orson? Try the radio."

There was a moment of quiet before Orson's voice came through the speaker. "Loud and clear!"

"Good." Sam was looking far too serious for first thing on a Monday. "I did some research over the weekend."

"Me too! There are a *lot* of monsters that eat children. Mostly for staying out late or disobeying their parents."

Sam glared at me until I stopped talking. "Anyway, I have a theory that the gelim is trapping Orson in the place where lost things go."

"That's what we think too," I said. I hadn't had much time to talk to Sam on Friday, so Orson and I filled her in on his theory about the gelim being like a spider who fed on fear, and I even told her about the poem carved into the church wall.

"Plus," I said, "Miss DeVore told me students have been complaining about the school being haunted since forever. Some of those stories are probably about the gelim, but what if others are about the boys it lured over there? What if the monster is the reason they got lost, *and* why they never found their way home?"

139

"So the monster lures boys to the place where lost things go, traps them there, and then feeds on their fear," Sam said. "If that's true, then it makes sense that Orson isn't the first."

"How do I escape?" Orson asked.

Sam's shoulders slumped. "I don't know yet. But I'm working on it, I promise."

The idea that the gelim might have been feeding off the students of St. Lawrence's for decades made me want to throw up. We had to stop the gelim, but I had no idea how or even where to begin. The problem felt too big for the three of us alone. Who could we ask for help? Who would believe us?

The bell rang.

"Come on," Sam said. "We'll talk more about this later, at lunch."

We said goodbye to Orson and left the library. As I lined up with the 6W class to go inside, I spotted Blake standing with Conrad. I couldn't stop staring at them, watching them laugh the way Blake and I used to laugh.

"You know it was Blake who put your stuff in the toilet Friday, right?"

I found Gordi standing beside me with his hands in his pockets. "How?" I asked, pretending I didn't already know. "He was running with me all period."

"Conrad did it for him. Got a bathroom pass and snuck into the locker room."

Blake knew my locker combination, so he'd probably given it to Conrad. "Why are you telling me? I thought you were his friend."

Gordi gave a half-hearted shrug. "I figured you guys would make up eventually, but Blake's not the same. He's meaner."

"You didn't seem to mind when you were holding my arms for him behind the church."

"I told Blake it wasn't cool!"

"But you did it anyway," I said.

Gordi hung his head. "Yeah. Sorry about that. Look, just watch your back, okay?" He moved away from me to the rear of the line like he was nervous Blake might see him talking to me, but as long as Conrad was whispering in his ear, I didn't exist.

─ ─ ─ ─ ─ ─

I'd only been stuck in detention for a week, but when I returned to the cupcakes' table, everything had changed. For one, Sam was sitting in my regular seat. For another, Paul, Trevor, Jackson, and Matt weren't spread out and keeping to themselves. They were sitting close together and were talking to each other. I took an empty seat across from Sam, sulking.

"You're back!" Sam said. "Lunch has been boring without you."

I glanced around the table. "Doesn't look like it."

"Did you know that Paul's mom worked for NASA?" Sam said. "And Trevor's got a half brother who writes detective novels."

Matt looked ruefully across the table. "No one in my family does anything interesting."

I knew I shouldn't feel jealous, but Sam had only been there a week, and she already had more friends than I did. It wasn't that I didn't like Matt, Trevor, Paul, and Jackson. I guess I'd just seen my time sitting with the cupcakes as temporary. I hadn't expected I'd become one.

"Hey," Sam said to the others, "what do you know about Conrad Eldridge?"

I stopped chewing and caught Sam's eye. She gave me a look that seemed to say, *Calm down. I have a plan.*

Jackson was the first to speak up. "I know enough to stay away from him."

"Yeah," Trevor said. "Isn't he buddies with your best friend, Hector?"

"Blake's not my best friend anymore," I mumbled.

"Remember when Clay got suspended last year for breaking into the church collection box?" Paul said. "I heard it was really Conrad who did it, but he blamed it on Clay."

"He did that to me!" Matt said. "He said I wrote something bad about Mrs. Ford on the wall in the restroom."

"Did you?" Trevor asked.

"No way." Matt was shaking his head. "I didn't get in trouble because there was no proof, but Mrs. Ford has hated me ever since."

"Mrs. Ford hates everyone," Trevor said.

Sam was watching each of them as they spoke, paying close attention. "So Conrad's always been a bully?"

Jackson took a drink from his water and then said, "But all the teachers think he's a saint. Saint Conrad. Nothing ever sticks to him."

"I bet he beat up the other babies in the hospital where he was born," Paul said, "and blamed it on the nurses."

I wasn't sure what Sam was trying to prove—I already knew Conrad was a jerk—but before I could ask her, Colonel Musser, along with Coach Barbary and Principal O'Shea, marched into the cafeteria and wove through the tables, finally stopping at Blake's. Everyone turned to see what was going on. Coach, Musser, and O'Shea loomed over Blake. I couldn't hear what they were saying, but even Principal O'Shea looked angry.

Conrad leaned over and whispered something to Blake that made him laugh. Coach Barbary pulled Blake to his feet by his collar. Blake's lips twisted into a scowl and his cheeks flushed red. He threw his hands in the air and pointed at me while shouting, "I didn't do it!"

Colonel Musser, her eyebrow arched so high it was practically at her hairline, shook her head and herded Blake toward the door. Coach picked up Blake's backpack, and Principal O'Shea said something to the rest of the boys at the table before leaving.

"What do you think *that* was about?" Paul asked. "And how much do you wanna bet Conrad was involved?"

I didn't know the answer to either question, but I had a feeling I was going to find out soon enough.

# 26

EVERYONE WAS WHISPERING about what happened to Blake during lunch. I expected to see him in the hallway when we changed classes between sixth and seventh periods, but he wasn't there. I peeked in Musser's room, and she still looked mad enough to chew sand and spit glass, but I wasn't nearly daring enough to ask her why.

After school, I was tempted to bike to Blake's house and ask him if he was okay, but I doubted he would've told me. Instead, I hid out and practiced piano while Mom was making dinner. Usually, Pop and the boys stayed away when I was practicing, so I was surprised when Pop stuck his head in the room and asked me to take a ride to the grocery store with him. I didn't want to go, but even though Pop made it sound like a question, I didn't think he was actually giving me a choice.

Pop sang along to the country song on the radio. He had

a voice like a rusty engine, and when he didn't know the words to the song, he made them up. We didn't need much from the store and were in and out quickly, but instead of heading right home, Pop took the scenic route along the beach and pulled off on the side of the road.

"Your mom's worried about you, Hector." Pop turned toward me, draping his arm over the steering wheel.

I didn't know what to say, so I just muttered, "I'm fine."

"Jason and Lee are easy to understand, because they're like me when I was their age, but you're a tough nut to crack."

"I don't mean to be."

For some reason, that made Pop smile. "You're a lot like your mom. She's so smart that I have trouble figuring out what she's thinking, and I need her to explain it to me sometimes."

"Okay," I said.

Pop drummed his fingers on the steering wheel. He looked uncomfortable, like he would have rather been anywhere else than stuck in that car with me.

"I guess what I'm saying is that even though I might have a tough time understanding what you're going through, I still want you to tell me. You might need to explain it slowly and use small words, though." Pop grinned and I couldn't help smiling back.

"It's just . . ."

"Hard being eleven?"

"Yeah."

Pop nodded knowingly. "Wait until you turn thirteen."

"Do I have to?"

"Eventually," Pop said. "Though your mom would prefer you didn't."

Pop was making an effort, and I felt like I had to tell him something. "I swear I'm not trying to get in trouble or upset you and Mom."

"Does it have anything to do with that boy Blake?"

I nodded.

"Is he more than a friend?" Pop asked. "Because it would be okay if he were."

I looked away. "He's not even my friend anymore."

Pop was quiet for a moment. Finally he clapped my shoulder. "I think I understand."

"You do?"

"Christine Fink."

"Who's that?" I asked.

"I gave her a Valentine's Day card in fifth grade, and she told everyone she'd seen me pick my nose and eat the boogers."

"Ew! Pop!"

"It wasn't true," Pop said, "but everyone believed her, so kids called me Booger the rest of the year. I nearly flunked grade five."

"Blake called me something worse than booger. A lot worse."

Pop pursed his lips. "If I tell your mom, she'll likely call Blake's moms."

"It won't do any good."

"I figured." Pop started the engine and pulled back onto the road. "Listen, Hector. I believe in standing up for yourself and facing your bullies, but there's no shame in asking for help, either. Everyone needs help sometimes. Got it?"

"Thanks, Booger."

Pop snorted and laughed.

Talking to Pop hadn't solved anything—I still didn't know what to do about Blake or the gelim or Mom—but I did feel a little bit better.

# 27

AFTER POP DROPPED me off at school, I went to the library to meet Sam, but the door was locked, which was unusual. Mr. Morhill was *always* at school early. I leaned over the hedges to peek through the windows, but the inside of the library was dark. When I turned around, Blake was standing at the bottom of the steps, flanked by Evan Christopher and Conrad Eldridge, who had his hands in his pockets. The muscle along Blake's jaw was twitching, and his eyes were puffy like he'd been crying all night.

"I know it was you, *freak*."

I backed up against the door. There was nowhere to run. "What was me?" I was proud my voice didn't tremble.

Conrad whispered something into Blake's ear that made his lip curl into a cruel smile. "How'd you do it? I didn't think you had it in you."

Evan Christopher stood uneasily, like he wasn't sure

what they were doing or if he wanted to be there, but Blake and Conrad formed an impenetrable wall.

"I swear, I don't know what you're talking about."

Blake spit on the ground at my feet. "My gym locker door just *happened* to be unlocked and open, and Coach Barbary just *happened* to wander by and see something inside that looked like it didn't belong, and it just *happened* to be some stupid bracelet belonging to Colonel Musser." Blake moved toward me as he spoke.

"I still don't—" Nothing Blake was saying made sense.

"O'Shea called my moms." Blake shoved me. "They took away my PlayStation." He shoved me again. "I'm grounded for a month, and I'll be stuck in detention even longer!" Blake pushed me harder, but there was nowhere to go, so I kept hitting the door.

"Please, Blake, I'm telling you I don't know what you're talking about!"

"They think I'm a thief," Blake said, "but I didn't steal *anything*. So how did Colonel Musser's bracelet end up in my locker?"

"Hey! What's going on?"

I'd never been so happy to see Jason in my life. He jogged toward us, his face red and sweaty from playing basketball.

Blake turned around and stood tall. "Your brother's a thief and a liar." Conrad whispered into Blake's ear. "Right. And a *freak*, too."

"Dude," Evan said. "Come on."

Jason's face paled and he squared his shoulders. "Don't talk about Hector like that."

"Why?" Blake said. "It's true, isn't it?"

Jason motioned at Conrad. "What are you doing hanging out with a sixth grader? Is it because everyone in our class thinks you're a creep?"

Conrad grinned and shrugged as he took a step toward Jason. Normally, I would've bet on Jason in a fight—he had a lot of experience wrestling with Lee and Pop—but Conrad struck me as the kind of boy who didn't fight fair and would do anything to win.

Blake hiked his thumb over his shoulder at me. "You know he nearly got me suspended? Stole a bracelet from Colonel Musser and planted it in my locker."

"I did not!" I said. "I told you I don't know what you're talking about!"

"I don't care what your problem is with Hector," Jason said. "Stay away from him. All of you."

"You gonna make me?" Blake stepped forward to stand beside Conrad.

Behind me, the library door unlocked, and I moved out of the way a second before it opened. Mr. Morhill stuck his head out and took in the scene. "Is there a problem here, Mr. Nesbitt?"

Conrad whispered into Blake's ear, and Blake said, "Nope." He, Conrad, and Evan took off toward the main building.

Jason waited until they were gone and then caught my

eye and nodded before leaving. I dashed inside to the safety of the library.

Mr. Morhill busied himself turning on the lights while I sat down and tried to figure out what had just happened.

"Sorry for running late this morning. Sam won't be at school today."

"Is she okay?"

"Nothing to concern yourself with." When Mr. Morhill was done with the lights, he stood at the circulation desk, folded his hands in front of him, and turned his full attention to me. "Would you care to explain what was going on outside?"

I shook my head.

"I'd like to help you, Mr. Griggs, but I can't if you don't trust me."

I didn't want to talk. Not to Mr. Morhill. Not to anyone. I stood and motioned toward the music room. "Piano" was all I could muster the energy to say. Mr. Morhill didn't try to stop me.

As scared as I was of the gelim, it was nothing compared to how I'd felt with Blake outside. He looked like the person who'd been my best friend, but he wasn't the same. I felt like my world had turned upside down. Before I'd asked Blake to be my boyfriend, *he* was the one who would have stood up to a bully like Conrad, and he never would have called me that terrible name. Instead I'd been rescued by Jason, who I'd assumed would have happily watched Conrad beat me up.

I played the piano in the music room until the bell rang and then went to stand with my class. I kept my eyes down so I could get through the day without stumbling over any more trouble. It was going fine until science. I trudged into Colonel Musser's room, took my seat, and put my head down on my desk. When class began, I looked up to where Musser was diagramming the internal structure of a cell on the whiteboard so she didn't yell at me for sleeping. That's when I saw it. Colonel Musser was wearing a silver bangle set with a turquoise stone.

That must have been the bracelet Blake was talking about, the one he'd been accused of stealing, and I'd seen it before.

My hand shot into the air, and I asked for a bathroom pass. "It's an emergency."

Colonel Musser scowled but sent me on my way. As soon as I was in the hallway, I ran to the restroom.

"Orson?" I turned invisible.

"Hector!" Orson strolled into the restroom, a big grin on his face. "I've been following you around all morning, I have so much—

"What did you *do*?" I said accusingly.

Orson stopped speaking. His smile slipped and he looked confused. "I don't—"

"You showed me the bangle! You said it belonged to Musser. How did it end up in Blake's locker?"

Orson's shoulders fell. "He dumped your stuff in the toilet. I was just getting even for what he did to you."

"Blake thinks *I* did it!" I was practically shouting, but I wasn't worried anyone would hear me. "You made everything worse!"

"Hector, I—"

"Just leave me alone." I turned visible and stormed out of the restroom.

— — — — — —

At lunch, Blake was all anyone could talk about. No one knew exactly what he'd done to get in trouble the day before, but there were a lot of rumors.

"I heard he stole money from Mrs. Ford," Trevor said.

Paul was shaking his head. "He told Father Allison in confession that he cheated on a couple of tests."

Matt smacked Paul's arm. "Priests don't tell anyone what you admit to in confession." He looked around the table. "Right?"

Blake was the last person I wanted to talk about. Even if Orson thought he was helping me, I never would have been okay with framing Blake for a crime he didn't commit. I wished there were a way for me to clear Blake's name without making myself look guilty, but Colonel Musser wouldn't believe me if I said an invisible boy—who'd disappeared three years ago and now lived in a weird place where lost things went—had found the silver bangle and planted it in Blake's locker as payback for Blake having his creepy eighth-grade friend stuff my backpack in the gym toilet.

Orson had no right to interfere. I didn't even know *how* he'd gotten the bracelet in the locker. The last time I'd seen it had been in the church. It shouldn't have been possible for Orson to move the bangle to the real world, yet he admitted he'd done it.

"Hey," Jackson said, nudging me with his foot under the table. "Where's Sam today?"

I shrugged. "Sick?"

"Oh."

The way they all looked disappointed by Sam's absence annoyed me. "How come none of you ever talked to me before Sam came along?"

Paul took a sip from his water bottle. "Why didn't *you* ever talk to us?"

"Fair question," I said. "But it's not like you guys talked to each other, either. Then Sam comes along, and you're suddenly best friends."

Jackson said, "It's easier to be friends with someone who doesn't know why everyone else thinks you're a weirdo."

"*I* don't know why people think you're weird."

Jackson pursed his lips. "Maybe because you never bothered to ask." It felt like an accusation. Either way, he was right. All I'd known was that this was the table where the cupcakes sat. I didn't know why people called them that, and I hadn't cared enough to find out.

"I'm asking now," I said.

A quiet fell over the table until Paul raised his hand

and said, "Apparently, I'm a sissy because I dance ballet and paint my nails."

Trevor added, "I have asthma and can't play sports."

Paul leaned over to look at Trevor. "Is *that* why the boys call you Wheezy?"

"I hate that nickname," Trevor muttered.

I turned to Jackson for his answer, and he returned a scary-good impression of Musser's disappointed eyebrow raise. "Because I like sports but I suck at most of them, because I won't let anyone touch my hair, because I bring food for lunch that y'all think is weird, because I don't live in the same part of town as the rest of you. Take your pick."

"Oh," I said. "Well, those are silly reasons."

"They're *all* silly reasons," Paul said.

I bet Orson had felt the same way as Jackson when he was visible. Like the other students saw him but they didn't really *see* him.

The other boys looked at Matt, who was quietly eating his lunch. Finally, Matt glared at them and said, "Fine! In fourth grade, I had a sleepover for Halloween, and I wet the bed. But it was only because I drank an entire liter of root beer on a dare right before going to sleep. Happy now?"

None of the reasons the boys had given seemed like things that should have made them outcasts. Who cared what happened in the third or fourth grade? And what was wrong with having painted nails or dancing ballet?

"I asked Blake to be my boyfriend," I said. "He called me a bad name, and I set his science project on fire."

"Whoa." Matt's eyes got huge.

Jackson said, "He could've just said 'No thank you.'"

I laughed. "That's what I said!"

The boys all began talking at once, asking how I'd set Blake's project on fire, why I'd wanted Blake to be my boyfriend, and if he was responsible for stuffing my belongings in the gym toilet. As I was telling the story of how I got into Blake's backyard, Gordi crept toward our table.

"I'm not going anywhere with Blake," I said. "You can tell him that."

Gordi kept his eyes down as he shook his head. "I'm not here for him."

"Then what?"

"I . . ." Gordi looked at me. "Can I sit with you guys?"

My first instinct was to say no, but I didn't think Gordi would've asked if he'd had anywhere else to go, and I couldn't turn him away. I glanced at the others. When no one protested, I said, "Yeah. Everyone's welcome here."

# 28

SAM DIDN'T COME back to school until Friday, and it felt like the longest three days of my life. At home, I kept trying to talk to Jason, but he found a million ways to avoid me. I just wanted to know why he'd stood up for me to Blake and Conrad, when he usually acted like he wished I'd never been born. Not much changed at school. Blake glared at me but didn't speak to me, not even to call me names while we were running laps, which Coach resumed after Monday's break. I was still avoiding Orson and refused to turn invisible. I was too angry to care what his reasons were for framing Blake for stealing the bracelet. The only real change was at lunch, where I was getting to know the other boys. I wished I'd taken the time to talk to them sooner.

Friday morning, Sam was waiting for me in the library. "Are you okay?" I asked.

"Just a cold." Sam still sounded a little stuffy. "What did I miss?"

I filled Sam in on what had happened with Blake—how he'd been caught with the bangle belonging to Colonel Musser, and how Orson was the one who'd put it there. I left out the part where I'd yelled at Orson and told him to leave me alone.

"How did he do it?" Sam said when I finished. "I thought he couldn't affect things here."

"I don't know."

"Have you asked him?"

I shook my head, unable to look her in the eye.

Frowning, Sam grabbed the walkie-talkie from her backpack and turned it on.

"Finally!" Orson's voice came through the speaker with a screech. "Hector, I'm sorry! If I'd known you were going to get so mad, I wouldn't have done it!"

Sam looked back and forth from me to the walkie. "I'm lost. What's going on?"

"Please don't ignore me anymore, Hector. It's so lonely with no one to talk to, and I'll never do anything like that again. I swear."

Orson sounded miserable, and I felt bad for being so mean to him. He'd been alone a long time, and just when he finally had people to talk to again, I'd abandoned him. "You shouldn't have gotten Blake in trouble, but I'm sorry for yelling at you."

It was hard talking to Orson without being able to see

him. I looked over at Sam, and she must've known what I was thinking because she said, "Go on." I turned invisible. The second I did, Orson threw his arms around me and hugged me so tight it hurt.

"I'm sorry, Hector. Please don't leave me like that again. I won't mess with Blake anymore. I promise."

The last of my anger vanished. What Orson had done was wrong, but I couldn't stay mad at him for trying to help me. I hugged him back. "It's okay. We're good."

"Uh, Hector? Orson?"

I let go of Orson and turned visible again. "I'll explain later," I said to Sam.

"No, I think I get it." Her tone made me feel even guiltier for the way I'd treated Orson. "What I want to know, Orson, is *how* you got the bangle in Blake's locker in the first place."

There was a pause. I tried to imagine Orson's face, the way he pinched his lips when he was thinking. "If an item gets lost and winds up on this side," Orson said, "sometimes I can nudge it back to your side."

Sam glanced at me and shrugged. Then she said, "How did you open the locker door?"

"It was already open. I was planning to drop the bracelet in Blake's cubby in his homeroom, but I was running from the gelim—"

"The gelim was chasing you?" I said, feeling the hairs on the back of my neck rise.

"I thought it was," Orson said. "I felt it nearby. I got

turned around and ended up in the locker room, trying to stay away from it. Blake's locker door was open, so I figured it was as good a place as any."

"How did you know which locker was his?" Sam asked.

Orson's snort came through the walkie-talkie loud and clear. "I know every locker at this school. Do you have any idea how boring it is here? Alone? I get so bored that I even sit through Mrs. Ford's lectures sometimes just to feel like I'm part of your world."

Sam wrinkled her nose. "Yikes."

Before we got off track, I said, "What are we going to do about Blake?"

"I don't think there's anything we *can* do." Sam tapped her lips as she thought. "Besides, I'm more concerned about the gelim chasing Orson."

Orson's voice was quieter through the walkie-talkie. "It's been coming to the church more often at night. I can hear it through the windows, taunting me and calling my name. Sometimes it feels like it would be easier to let it get me—"

"Don't you dare!" I said. "Don't even think about it."

Orson didn't respond for a couple of seconds.

"You there?" Sam said. "Orson?"

Orson's voice came through finally. "I'm not giving up. It's just hard."

Even after everything Blake had done and said, I hated letting him take the blame for something he didn't do, but Sam was right. The gelim was the more immediate threat.

"Any ideas how to fight the monster and bring Orson back?"

"Actually, there's something I want to check," Sam said.

"What?" Orson and I said at the same time.

Sam pursed her lips. "I know it's dangerous with the gelim lurking about, but I need you to turn invisible, get into the file room, and leave it unlocked for me. Can you do that?"

"It won't work," Orson said.

"Why not?" Sam asked, and I was curious too.

The walkie-talkie crackled. "If the file room is locked on your side, it'll be locked on this side too."

I glanced at Sam and shrugged. "Sorry."

"Do you know who has the keys?"

"Well, Miss DeVore, but—"

"I could distract her," Orson said. "Then Hector could grab the keys, unlock the door, and return them before she notices."

"How are you going to do that?" I looked from Sam to where I'd last seen Orson, waiting for one of them to answer.

"Why don't *I* cause the distraction," Sam said. "I can get DeVore out of the office, Hector can steal the keys, and Orson can be the lookout."

It was a solid plan, and I only had one objection. "What about the gelim?" I couldn't help remembering the tentacle snaking out of the stairwell, its teeth sinking into my ankle.

"Hey," Orson said, "nothing's going to hurt you on my watch." I knew it was impossible, but I swore I could feel his hand on my back.

"What do you need the file room unlocked for anyway?" I said, looking at Sam.

"I have a theory I want to confirm," Sam said. "So, will you do it?"

Grabbing the keys and unlocking the door would only take a few seconds. I wouldn't be invisible long enough for the gelim to know I was there, and Orson would be watching my back. Nothing was going to hurt me. I hoped. "Yeah, I'm in."

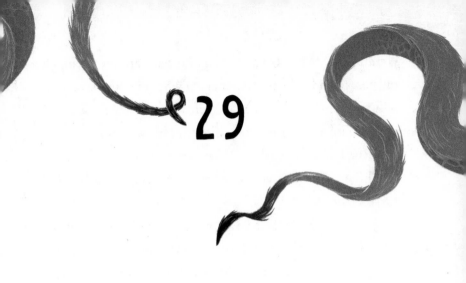

# 29

ORSON WAS WAITING for me in the stairwell at the end of the day. We hugged the wall outside the main office as the other boys dashed past on their way to the front of the building, where they'd meet their parents or get on the bus. Sam would be along soon to cause her diversion, but we didn't have much time. Jason was probably already outside waiting for Pop to pick us up.

"I'm sorry," Orson said suddenly.

"It's all right—"

Orson turned to face me. "No it's not. I shouldn't have set up Blake for stealing that bracelet." He sank to the carpet and pulled his knees to his chest. "I've been by myself so long, and ever since we met, I've been terrified of being alone again. I thought if I got even with Blake, it would make you like me enough to not leave."

I sat beside Orson, shoulder to shoulder. "I already like

you, Orson. We're friends. You and Sam are pretty much my best friends." I couldn't imagine what I would have been willing to do for friends if I'd been alone as long as Orson. I hoped Sam and I could help him find his way home.

"Really?" Orson asked. "Even after what I did?"

"Like it or not, you're stuck with me." I smiled and Orson laughed.

Finally, Sam jogged down the hall toward us. Outside Miss DeVore's office, she whispered, "I hope you guys are ready," before ducking in. "Miss DeVore! There's a second grader stuck in a tree! I need someone to help talk him down."

Orson snorted. "That's her best idea? A boy stuck in a tree?"

I shushed him even though no one could hear us.

"I don't know," Miss DeVore said. "That sounds like a job for Coach—"

"There's no time. Come on!"

A moment later Sam, followed by Miss DeVore, walked quickly out of the office. Now it was my turn. I became visible, snatched Miss DeVore's keys off her desk, became invisible again, and jogged back to where Orson was waiting. I unlocked the file room door and tested it to make sure it would remain unlocked. Then I ran back to Miss DeVore's office and returned her keys, hoping she wouldn't notice they'd been moved. I felt like a secret agent.

"Hey," I shouted to Orson. "Why do you think Sam wanted me to leave the file room unlocked?"

Orson didn't answer. When I came out of the office, he had his head cocked to the side like a dog listening for a sound too high for anyone else to hear, and he was shifting his weight back and forth from one foot to the other.

"What—"

"Hush." Orson put his finger to his lips. "Don't you feel that?" he whispered.

I hadn't noticed until he mentioned it, but the air did seem cooler. Damp. I was about to say so when a pair of tentacles snaked through the front doors. The tip of one smacked me in the chest and sent me flying backward into the wall, knocking the breath out of me.

I was dazed, and everything hurt, but Orson grabbed my arm and pulled it around his shoulders. "We gotta run, Hector!"

Orson half carried, half dragged me down the hall, away from the tentacles that were forcing their way inside. Two at first. Then three and four more squirmed in. The hungry mouths on the underside smacked their lips and gnashed their teeth. I could smell their breath. It was as bad as Jason's in the morning. But worse than the stink were the feelings that threatened to drown me. I was never going to escape. I was a failure. I was a loser. I belonged with the cupcakes. I was everything Blake said I was, and I couldn't change no matter how hard I tried.

"Leave me. Save yourself."

"No way," Orson said. "Don't let it get in your head."

I clung to Orson's voice. He'd eluded the gelim for years.

And if he could do it for that long, I could do it for a few more minutes. I focused on putting one foot in front of the other, leaning on Orson as much as I could without slowing him down.

We burst out the back, and Orson left me resting against the railing while he shut the doors.

"Gimme your belt," he said, sounding much calmer than I felt. My heart was thumping in my throat, and I wanted to throw up.

The tentacles pounded the doors, and Orson bounced off them before slamming his weight against them again. I fumbled with the buckle, slipped off my belt, and handed it over. Orson fed the belt through the handles and yanked it tight.

"It won't hold long," he said.

"The church?" I managed to say between breaths. The doors rattled as the gelim fought to break through them.

Orson shook his head. "I'll go to the church. You turn visible and get away."

"But—"

"You don't have to stay here," Orson said. "I do. No use both of us getting trapped."

The door stopped shaking.

"It's coming around the other side. I'll lure it away. Library. Monday morning." Without waiting for me to object, Orson sprinted toward the church.

I hated leaving, but Orson hadn't given me much choice. Maybe if I'd been braver, I would have chased him and we could have faced the gelim together. Instead I took off in the opposite direction, jogging around the side of the school toward student drop-off and pickup, where Pop was probably waiting for me, annoyed that I was late. Before I'd gone too far, I remembered my belt. Mom would be furious if I went home without it, and I didn't want to give her another reason to be angry with me. I crept back to the rear doors and nearly yelped when I spotted Conrad Eldridge looking around, sniffing the air.

I was still invisible, but I held my breath anyway, afraid to make a sound. There was something *off* about him. I mean, there was always something off about Conrad, but the longer I watched him, the more convinced I became that he was just *wrong*. I crept closer, remaining hidden, and that was when I realized what had been bothering me. Conrad didn't have a shadow! I moved around carefully, checking him out from all sides, but I was right. No shadow at all. But what did that mean? Orson said only objects that belonged in the place lost things went didn't have a shadow. Was Conrad invisible like me? Was *he* the gelim? That thought was too big to wrap my mind around. I needed to talk to Orson and Sam about it. A moment later, Conrad's head jerked up like he'd caught a scent, and he trotted off in the direction Orson had run.

I grabbed my belt from around the door handles and dashed toward the front of the school. I willed myself to turn visible, but nothing happened. I stopped and concentrated. I felt like I was being held in place with Velcro. I had to strain to tear myself free. I saw my reflection in the windows shimmer and vanish. Appear for a second and then disappear. I screwed my eyes shut and tried as hard as I could, one enormous push. I felt like I was being shucked like an ear of corn, but when I opened my eyes, I saw my reflection in the glass and breathed a sigh of relief.

I reached the front of the school, prepared for a lecture from Pop about being late, but instead of seeing Pop's squad car waiting for me, I watched it drive away.

"Pop! Where are you going?" I waved my arms and ran after him, but he didn't see me.

I trudged around to the front steps and sat down. I couldn't believe Pop had left. Why would he leave without me? Had Jason told him I'd gone home with someone else? Did they think Mom had picked me up for a dentist appointment? What else could possibly go wrong?

"Hector? What are you doing here? Didn't I just see your stepfather leave?" Colonel Musser stood over me, her long shadow shading me from the sun.

I nodded miserably.

Colonel Musser sat beside me. "Then I suppose we'll have to wait for him to realize his error together."

I couldn't think of anything to say. I hadn't even had time to process being chased by the gelim again, and now I was worried because Conrad Eldridge didn't have a shadow, even though I had no idea how that was possible or what it meant, *and* I'd had trouble turning visible. I didn't want to leave Orson alone in the land of lost things, but I was terrified of being trapped there with him.

"Is everything all right, Hector?"

I certainly couldn't tell her the truth. "I'm okay, I guess."

"You seem different. You *and* Mr. Nesbitt. You're sneaking out of class and making up stories about monsters; he's failing to turn in assignments, talking back, and . . ." Musser's voice trailed off, but she glanced at the bangle on her wrist. "You boys are friends, right?"

"We were."

"Ah." Colonel Musser didn't speak for a moment. It was weird hanging out with her. It was like she was a real person instead of just a teacher. "Have you ever heard of the double-slit experiment, Hector?"

"No, ma'am."

Colonel Musser cleared her throat. "The short version is that light has the properties of both particles and waves. The double-slit experiment proved that light still acts like a wave even when it's a solitary particle. They did this by firing light, one photon at a time, through a barrier with two slits on it for the photon to pass through."

"Weird," I said.

Musser chuckled. "The really strange part is that when scientists attempted to determine which slit the individual photons passed through, they stopped acting like waves."

"Really?" Even though science wasn't my best subject, Colonel Musser had a way of making it interesting.

"Really," Musser said. "The act of observing the photons changed how they behaved."

"Cool." And it was. I just didn't know what it had to do with anything.

"People are like those photons sometimes, Hector. They may act one way when they're alone and a different way when others are watching." Musser caught my eye. "Like how you boys have been calling me Colonel behind my back for two decades."

I hung my head and mumbled, "Sorry."

"It's only a name," Musser said.

"But bad names can hurt."

Musser nodded. "They can, but sometimes words have power only because we give it to them. You students calling me Colonel Musser doesn't bother me because I know that behind the laughter, you're all a little afraid of me."

I'd never thought about it like that. "But aren't there some names so bad you shouldn't ever use them?"

"There are," Musser said. "Has someone been calling you one of those names? Because we have a zero-tolerance policy for bullying."

"I . . ." I shut my mouth and bowed my head.

"It's difficult being different." Miss Musser sighed. "Trust me on this one. I know from experience."

"You do?"

She nodded. "But being called names for remaining true to who you are is still better than being popular for attempting to be someone you're not. Be proud of who you are, Hector Griggs, and one day the rest of the world will catch up."

Pop's police cruiser came barreling back toward school. Musser slapped her knee and stood. "Looks like your ride's here."

"Thanks, Miss Musser." I got up and headed toward the car. "And remember what I said about light particles, Hector."

As soon as I got in the car, Pop turned around. "Sorry about that, kiddo. We got all the way home before I realized you weren't in the back seat."

Jason was looking at me, his face scrunched up, more confused than normal.

"You forgot about me?"

Pop laughed it off. "You're usually so quiet, I'm surprised it doesn't happen more often."

"Funny," I said. But it wasn't funny at all.

As Pop pulled out of the lot, I spotted Conrad standing by the church being lectured by Father Carmichael.

"What're you looking at?" Jason asked.

"Just checking for something," I mumbled. Father Carmichael's shadow stretched out from his feet like the big hand of a clock, but Conrad didn't have a shadow at all. And since Father Carmichael could see him, it meant he wasn't invisible. He was something else entirely, but I didn't know what.

# 30

POP ORDERED PIZZA Friday night and even let me pick the toppings to apologize for forgetting me at school. We watched a superhero show as a family—Pop kept asking what everyone was saying until Mom finally turned on the subtitles, Jason made jokes throughout the whole show, and Lee was too busy texting with a girl to notice the rest of us existed. I felt more normal than I had since I'd first turned invisible in the church two weeks earlier. For one night, I tried not to think about Orson, the gelim, or what Conrad Eldridge's missing shadow meant. The one thing I couldn't stop thinking about was Musser's story and the way photons acted when no one was around. It gave me an idea.

Saturday morning, I rode my bike to Blake's house and knocked on the front door. One of his moms answered. I called her Mrs. N. and his other mom Mrs. Nesbitt.

"Hector? It's good to see you, sweetie. How's that smile of yours?" Mrs. N. was a dentist and obsessed with teeth.

"Is Blake home?"

Mrs. N. stood aside to let me in. "He's in his room."

If Miss Musser was right, then maybe the only chance I had of settling things with Blake was to do it where no one at school could overhear us. Maybe the only reason he acted the way he did was because other people were always around. That was my theory, anyway.

The problem was that Blake wasn't alone. I could hear him talking with someone, and I recognized the other voice. My first instinct was to become invisible so I could listen to what they were saying without being seen, but it would be wrong to spy on them *and* I was worried I wouldn't be able to turn back. I also considered leaving, but Mrs. N. would tell Blake I'd come by, and I didn't want him to think I was afraid of him. I was—I just didn't want *him* to know it. So, after considering my options, I marched into his room.

Blake and Evan Christopher turned around at the same time. They were sitting on the floor playing a racing video game. I guess Blake had convinced his moms to give him back his PlayStation. Evan smiled at me and waved, but Blake's lip curled and his nostrils flared.

"What're *you* doing here?" Blake said.

I'd never needed a reason to show up at Blake's house. Almost from the day we'd met, we'd practically lived at each other's houses. None of our parents questioned when

173

one of us showed up for dinner at the other's table. We'd been inseparable. Now I felt like an intruder.

Evan elbowed Blake and scowled at him. "Can't you stop fighting already? This is silly."

Blake snatched Evan's controller from his hand and threw it in the corner. "Shut up or go home."

Evan caught my eye for a second and then looked away.

I hung my head. "I shouldn't have come."

As I turned around, Blake said, "That's right. Run away, *freak*."

I stopped. I'd gone to Blake's house to say something, and I needed to say it even if he wasn't alone. "There's something wrong with Conrad Eldridge." I couldn't explain about him not having a shadow since I didn't understand it myself, but Blake deserved to know that the eighth grader wasn't what he seemed. "You shouldn't hang out with him."

Blake snorted. "So I should hang out with you and the cupcakes? No thanks."

"Please, Blake. Just listen—"

"*Please! Please!*" Blake whined. Then he laughed. "I know it was you who planted that bracelet in my locker, and you're gonna pay."

I turned to leave.

"Later, *freak!*"

Mrs. N. tried to talk to me when I got downstairs, but I had to get out of Blake's house before I started to cry.

I was sitting at the piano, trying to practice, when Mom found me later that day. She sat down beside me and draped her arm around my shoulders. It was the first time she'd really hugged me since our last fight, and I'd missed it.

"I just got off the phone with Nora Nesbitt."

"Oh." I could only imagine what Blake's mom had told mine.

"She said she and Melanie are worried about you. They haven't seen you around in a while, and then you left the house near tears." Mom paused. "You don't have to explain what's going on between you and Blake, but you can if you want to."

I couldn't tell my mom about Orson or Sam or the gelim or even about Conrad Eldridge, and I doubted she could help me with Blake, but maybe she *could* help me understand why he hated me so much.

"I asked Blake to be my boyfriend, and he got angry and called me a name."

Mom tensed up. "What name, Hector?"

I shook my head. "Please don't make me say it. And please don't tell his moms. It'll only make things worse."

Mom didn't respond, so I kept going.

"After he called me that name, I was so angry that I snuck into his backyard and set his science project on fire."

"Hector Myles Griggs!" Mom let go of me and turned to look me in the eye. "What were you thinking?"

"I wasn't! And I tried to apologize! I told him I was sorry, and I even offered to tell Miss Musser, but he wasn't interested."

Mom shut her eyes and took a deep breath. "We're going

to talk about you playing with fire, but for now let's set it aside. Why didn't you talk to me about this sooner?"

"Blake already hated me," I said. "I figured if I told you, you'd tell Mrs. N. and Mrs. Nesbitt, and then Blake would hate me even more."

"At least now I understand why you've been getting into so much trouble lately."

I wished I could tell her Blake was only half the reason. "But, Mom, *why* is Blake being so mean? That's what I don't understand."

Mom blew out a breath and ran her hand through her hair. "I suspect that he was scared of what the other boys at your school would think if they found out."

"Why?"

"Because people can be cruel to those who are different."

"There's nothing wrong with being different," I said. "Everyone's different in some way."

Mom's smile seemed sad. "It takes most people a long time to figure that out. Some never do. One of my favorite things about you, Hector, is that you already know it."

"So you think Blake's being mean to me because he doesn't want people to think he's different?"

"And it's possible he said what he did because he saw how much words like that hurt his moms and knew it would hurt you, too."

I hung my head. "I wish I'd never asked him to be my boyfriend."

Mom hugged me again. "Don't think that, Hector. Don't

ever let someone else's insecurities stop you from following your heart."

I let Mom hug me for a while because I felt safe and loved, and after everything that had happened, I needed that. When I'd finished soaking up my mom's hug, I said, "What can I do to fix things with Blake?"

Mom squeezed me tighter. "I'm not sure you can. I suspect this is something he's going to have to work through on his own."

That wasn't the answer I was hoping for. "So I should leave him alone?"

"For now," she said. "But that doesn't mean you have to give up on him. You keep being you, and one day he might come around."

"I hope so."

"Me too, Hector. Me too."

# 31

SUNDAY MORNING, MOM made waffles the way I liked them, with whipped cream and strawberries on top, and when Jason complained that he liked pancakes better, she told him he was old enough to make them himself if he wanted them so badly. He glared at me the whole time he was eating his waffles, which made my breakfast taste even better. I was practicing piano later that day when Mom told me there was someone at the door for me. I ran to the living room, hoping it was Blake, but it was Sam instead.

"It's not every day someone looks that disappointed to see me," Sam said.

"I thought you'd be someone else."

"Sometimes I am. Today I'm just me." Sam flashed a smile. "Can you talk?"

"Mom!" I shouted through the house. "I'm going outside

with my friend Sam!" I left before she could come and ask Sam a hundred questions. "How'd you get here?"

Sam motioned at her bike, which was leaning against the mailbox. "I figured out we don't live too far from each other when Uncle Archie dropped you off that time. Took no time at all to get here."

We walked to the end of the driveway and turned left, wandering down the street. It was a cloudy day but still warm, and sweat beaded on my forehead.

"I spent the day in the file room yesterday, and I found something disturbing." She glanced at me. "Thanks for unlocking it, by the way. I watched a YouTube video about how to pick locks, but I'm not sure I could've done it. Did you run into any trouble?"

I snorted. "More like ran *from* trouble." I told Sam about borrowing Miss DeVore's keys, about the gelim, and about Conrad Eldridge, but I left out the part where I had trouble turning visible and Pop forgot about me. I didn't want to give her anything else to worry over.

Sam was quiet for a while after I finished. Then she said, "I'm so sorry, Hector. I never meant to put you in danger."

"It wasn't your fault."

"Do you think Orson is okay?"

"He survived there for a long time before he met us."

Sam nodded. She seemed lost in thought, and I hated to disturb her, but I had urgent questions.

"What do you think it means that Conrad doesn't have a shadow?"

"I don't know," Sam said. "But it kind of has to do with what I came to talk to you about and why I needed you to unlock the file room. Remember when we discussed Orson not being the first boy to disappear? Well, I went through the student records looking for a pattern, and I found one. I'm pretty sure boys have been vanishing from St. Lawrence's almost since the school was founded."

I stopped and stared at her. "For real?"

"Miss DeVore is a meticulous record keeper, but there are files—at least one boy every five years—that just stop. No transfer, no reason listed for them leaving school. The thing that connects the boys is that they were having trouble in school. Maybe some were being bullied; maybe others were struggling to fit in. But I believe the gelim used their loneliness to encourage them to fall between the cracks into the place where lost things go."

"So the gelim's been snatching boys from the school for seventy years?" I did the math in my head. "That would be about fifteen boys." All those boys, gone. Forgotten about. No one to wonder what happened to them. No one to miss them.

"I think I found fourteen," Sam said. "Not including you."

"But Orson only disappeared three years ago. Why is it after me now?"

Sam just shrugged. "There's one more thing, though."

I was afraid to ask. "What?"

"There's no file on Conrad at all."

I frowned. "Maybe Miss DeVore has it at her desk?"

Sam shook her head. "I looked. There is no student at St. Lawrence's by the name of Conrad Eldridge, and I'm not sure there ever was."

I'd been circling a possibility all weekend, afraid to admit it to anyone else, but Sam's revelation gave me the courage to say it out loud. "Do you think *Conrad* could be the gelim?"

Sam's eyes widened. "It's possible. I was actually thinking he was like you, able to move between the lost place and here."

"Conrad is nothing like me. Anyway, he wasn't invisible when I saw him. Check for yourself if you don't believe me." I looked down at my own shadow stretching out behind me to reassure myself it was there. "Conrad's the monster. He has to be. It makes perfect sense." The idea of the monster wandering around school wearing Conrad like a costume made it even more terrifying than before.

"We don't know anything for sure, and we shouldn't jump to conclusions. If the gelim can exist in our world and can look human, then it could be anyone. Don't tell me you can't see Mrs. Ford eating children without feeling guilty."

"Fair point," I said. "But even if Conrad isn't the monster, he still doesn't have a shadow, and . . ." I thought about all the times I'd seen Conrad whispering in Blake's ear.

"What is it, Hector?"

"If Conrad's the gelim, then maybe he's doing something to Blake. Maybe *Conrad* is the reason Blake's been acting the way he has. That's got to be it. Conrad's been poisoning him, making him act like a creep, and if we can convince him to leave, Blake will go back to the way he was before."

"Back up a second." There was a sadness in Sam's eyes. "It's possible Blake's behavior is the gelim's fault, or the gelim might have tapped into anger that was already inside him. Either way, we don't know Conrad is the monster, and it's dangerous to assume anything without proof."

I felt so certain I was right, and nothing Sam could say was going to change my mind. "Blake wasn't cruel before he started hanging out with Conrad. If we get rid of Conrad, I'll get Blake back again." I just had to figure out how.

# 32

MONDAY MORNING IN the library, Sam and I filled Orson in on everything we'd learned. Before, we'd only speculated that Orson wasn't the first to go missing, but now we had proof. I wished our proof about Conrad being the monster were equally solid.

"I don't know," Orson said through the walkie-talkie. "I'm kind of with Sam on this one."

Sam threw me a look that wasn't quite *I told you so*, but was close enough to be annoying.

"How do you explain him not having a shadow when he wasn't invisible, though? And he just happened to show up at the back door right after the gelim couldn't get through? What about the way he's always whispering in Blake's ear? Conrad's the reason Blake's been acting strange, I'm sure of it!" Even if he wasn't *the* monster, he was definitely *a* monster.

Sam rested her hand on my shoulder. "I get that this is important to you, but we can't accuse Conrad of being the gelim without proof."

"Besides," Orson chimed in, "what would we do if we had proof? Not like we can take it to the monster police."

I felt like they were ganging up on me. "Don't you want to come home, Orson?"

"Well, yeah—"

I turned to Sam. "And didn't you say you thought the gelim was the reason Orson was stuck on the other side?"

"That's true," she said.

"Then we have to confront it."

Orson snorted. "Have you forgotten the tentacles, Hector? What about the teeth? The gelim's got a lot of both."

"Why don't we talk to it here, when it looks like Conrad, instead of on the other side when it's all tentacles and teeth?"

"That's a terrible idea," Orson said at the same time as Sam said, "That's an excellent idea!"

Then Sam and Orson began arguing about whether it was the worst idea I'd ever had or the best. I was on the fence. The only thing I knew for sure was that we had to do something if we were going to rescue Orson and save my best friend. Even though Sam liked my idea, I suspected she'd still want to confirm Conrad was definitely the gelim before we confronted him, so I proposed a plan.

"One of us should follow Conrad to get proof he's the monster I think he is."

Sam stopped bickering with Orson long enough to stare at me. "Are you volunteering?" she asked. "Because I think it might be too dangerous—"

"I'll do it." Orson sounded braver over the walkie-talkie than I felt.

"You don't have to," I said.

"It's all right." I could picture Orson shrugging. "Watching y'all is boring, anyway."

I admired Orson's courage even as I felt relieved I wouldn't have to spend time shadowing Conrad. "Okay, so Orson's on Conrad duty. What do we do if I'm right and Conrad *is* the gelim? We need a plan so we can talk to him without being interrupted."

"*Talk* to him?" Sam said.

I nodded. "We can't hurt the gelim, but maybe we can reason with it. If we convince Conrad he's outnumbered, maybe he'll let Orson go. We might even be able to persuade him to leave the school."

Neither Sam nor Orson sounded optimistic about my idea, but they didn't argue, either. We decided that while waiting for Orson to get proof that Conrad was the gelim, Sam and I should go about our lives like normal to avoid alerting Conrad that we were onto him.

But we weren't the only ones who were up to something. I should have suspected the worst when I saw the eighth graders returning late from PE. They were sweatier than normal, flushed and walking off the field like they barely had the strength to stand. Even Jason looked beat.

"Listen up, boys," Coach Barbary said to us, standing with his meaty arms crossed over his chest. A whistle dangled from a cord around his bull neck. He looked pleased with himself, and that scared me. "This week we'll be performing a series of athletic drills designed to test your overall physical fitness. You'll receive points based on your performance, which will be tallied and used to rank you against the other boys."

Nearly everyone groaned.

"This is *not* a competition," Coach Barbary said. "But it's important for you to know where you stand in relation to your peers." He pointed at a ten-gallon cooler by the wood fence. "I want you to stay hydrated, so drink plenty of water when you need it."

It was never a good sign when an adult warned us to stay hydrated. The last time it had happened to me was when Pop had made me try out for flag football with Jason. Between the water, the heat, and the pancakes I'd had for breakfast, I'd ended up puking on my cleats.

Coach had us do push-ups until we couldn't, followed by sit-ups, pull-ups, jumping jacks, and burpees. By the end of class, my arms felt like worn-out rubber bands. Of course, Blake had had no problem with any of the exercises. He had probably done best in every category, while I'd definitely performed the worst.

On Tuesday, Coach forced us to run, climb, and crawl our way through an obstacle course he'd designed. We ran it one at a time while the rest of the class watched and cheered—or in some cases jeered.

I'd never liked PE, but by Wednesday I absolutely dreaded it. Though Coach hadn't put up the rankings yet, everyone knew Blake was at the top and I was at the bottom, and it was making him unbearable. The only thing that kept me going was the hope that Orson would turn up proof Conrad was the monster so we could free Blake from the gelim's spell. So far, he'd found nothing.

On Friday Coach Barbary announced that our last activity would be long-distance running. After changing, as I was heading toward the field, Coach clapped me on the back and said, "Those rankings aren't set in stone, Hector. It's a good thing you've been practicing."

Even though I was annoyed at Coach Barbary for acting like the laps he'd had me running the last couple of weeks were a favor instead of punishment, I was grateful for an event where I might not come in last. When everyone was ready, Coach blew the starting whistle. Some of the boys, like Gordi and Evan and Matt, sprinted off the line, pulling ahead of the others early, but they barely made it a mile before they had to drop out with side stitches and cramps. I didn't have to be the fastest runner on the track, I only had to outlast the other boys, so I fell into a familiar rhythm, ignoring everyone around me. I focused on putting one foot in front of the other. I could run all day.

One by one, the boys gave up from thirst or exhaustion,

and as the end of the period neared, Blake and I were the only boys remaining. He'd been a little ahead of me for most of the race, but he slowly dropped back until we were jogging side by side.

"Quit now, Hector. You're never gonna beat me."

"I don't care about beating you." My thighs burned, my feet hurt, and it was tough to keep my breath steady. "I just want my best friend back."

"*Freak*," Blake muttered. "How about this: you tell everyone you put that bracelet in my locker and I'll let you win."

"Only if you stop hanging out with Conrad Eldridge." I shouldn't have been wasting precious breath talking.

Blake snorted. "What? And come hang out at the cupcake table with you? No thanks."

We were on the far end of the track, but I could hear a few boys chanting Blake's name. I doubted they even cared if he won. They just wanted him to beat *me*.

"The only reason I was ever friends with you," Blake said, "was because I felt sorry for you. No one here likes you. Even your own stepbrother hates you. He said his dad marrying your mom was the worst thing that ever happened to him."

I stumbled but managed to stay upright. "Jason never said that."

Blake was smirking. "You sure?"

I wasn't, because it sounded like something Jason might've said. My strength began to falter. Why should

I keep running when Blake was going to win either way? For that matter, why should I bother talking to Conrad Eldridge when Blake didn't want to be helped? Maybe my mom was right, and there was nothing I could do for Blake. Maybe I should quit before I embarrassed myself.

"Last lap!" Coach Barbary called as we came around. "First to the finish line wins!"

The boys were cheering for Blake, shouting his name. But then I heard it. "Go for it, Hector!" Someone was cheering for *me*. It was Gordi. He was standing with Paul and Matt and Evan. They were all calling my name. As we jogged past them, a few more boys took up the chant. Not as many as were rooting for Blake, but hearing my name reminded me that I wasn't alone.

"You can't do it," Blake said at the halfway point. "You're weak. You can't beat me, and you can't beat *him*."

There was nothing more for me to say. I dug deep for my last crumbs of strength. I probably wouldn't be able to move for the entire weekend, but I wasn't going to give in to Blake Nesbitt.

As we made the final turn, the bleachers blocked our view of Coach and the rest of the class. Blake drifted toward me and stuck out his foot. I was running one second, and then I was tumbling. I hit the dirt. First my knee, then my elbow and shoulder. Explosions of pain flashed across my body. The world tilted sideways. I was dazed—unsure, at first, what had happened. I slowly got to my feet, wincing. Blood dribbled down my arms and legs. I looked up in time to watch Blake cross the finish line, raising his arms over his head, victorious.

No one had seen Blake trip me, so I'd only look like a sore loser if I told Coach. It hadn't been enough for Blake to beat me; he'd had to humiliate me too. Maybe it should have made me feel better that Blake had needed to cheat to win, but it didn't.

I didn't bother finishing the race. I stood, brushed myself off, and walked straight from the track to the locker room so that no one would see me cry.

# 33

**"IT'S NOT FAIR,"** Paul said at lunch. "We all know he tripped you."

Everyone, including Sam, who hadn't even been there, agreed. Evan had joined our table that day without asking. He'd just shown up, taken a seat beside Gordi, and acted like he ate lunch with us every day. He even offered up a bag of M&M's from his lunch for the table to share.

"When did Blake become such a bully?" Gordi asked.

"Ever since he started hanging out with Conrad," Evan said.

Jackson coughed, and we turned to look at him.

"What?" I said.

"Spit it out," Sam said.

Now that Jackson had the table's full attention, he looked like he wished he didn't. "Well, it's just that Blake's always kind of been a little bit of a bully."

I shook my head. "That's not true."

Paul nodded, and I thought he was agreeing with me, but he said, "Jackson's right. I mean, he wasn't like he is *now*, but sometimes he could be cruel without realizing it."

I couldn't believe what they were saying. "You've got it wrong. It's Conrad who's making Blake act like a jerk."

Matt elbowed Trevor. "Remember when he wouldn't leave you alone after you got poison oak?"

"But Blake was only joking," I said.

Trevor shrugged. "Wasn't funny to me."

After that, the floodgates broke open. The cupcakes all had stories about times Blake had made fun of them. Even Evan and Gordi joined in with a couple. It was like they were talking about a totally different person from the Blake I'd known. When I couldn't listen anymore, I pushed back my chair and stood.

"Wait, Hector," Sam said. "Where are you going?"

"Restroom." I limped to the out-of-order restroom so I could be alone.

My elbows and knees ached. Coach had sent me to the nurse's office, but there hadn't been much she could do except clean and bandage the scrapes. I turned invisible and found Orson leaning against the wall. He busted out a grin when he saw me, but I didn't smile back.

"Did you hear what they said? How could they think Blake was a bully?"

Orson folded his arms over his chest. "Maybe you didn't see it because he was your best friend. Or maybe you don't want to believe it because you're thinking that if Blake was a bully before he started hanging out with Conrad, then those things he said when you asked him to be your boyfriend weren't because of the monster."

That couldn't be true. The only reason Blake called me that name was because the gelim made him. "You don't know what you're talking about. Why are you even following me? Aren't you supposed to be watching Conrad?"

"It's lunch. He's not going to reveal himself as the gelim here." Orson was quiet for a moment. "Listen, I'm not saying Blake was a mean person before, but it's possible he wasn't always nice, either."

"Then what's the point of saving him from Conrad?" I threw up my hands. "What's the point of any of this?"

Orson coughed. "I mean, you're helping me, too."

Here I was upset about Blake being called a bully, while Orson was literally fighting for his life. "I didn't mean . . . Of course I want to help you, too. I'm sorry. It's just been a terrible day and—"

"I get it, Hector. But so what if Blake wasn't always the best person before? Doing the right thing is a choice. The gelim whispering in his ear is robbing him of the ability to make his own decisions."

"But what if we convince Conrad to leave Blake alone, and he still chooses to be a jerk?"

Orson shrugged with his hands. "Then at least you know you've done everything you can to help him."

I hung my head. "It feels so hopeless, Orson."

Orson slung his arm around my shoulders. "There were plenty of times over the last three years I thought about letting the gelim catch me. Wanna know what kept me going?"

"I guess," I mumbled.

"Chicken pot pie."

I snorted. "Chicken pot pie?"

Orson rubbed his belly. "My mom makes the best chicken pot pie in the whole world. She bakes these biscuits that are so flaky and buttery they melt in your mouth." He wiped imaginary drool from his lips.

I couldn't help laughing. "I don't think Blake knows how to make biscuits."

"All I'm saying is you have to find a reason to not give up, even if it's as silly as chicken pot pie."

Maybe Orson was right. Maybe it didn't matter who Blake had been or who he was. Each new day offered us the chance to be better people than we were the day before. All we had to do was choose it. I needed to know what kind of person Blake would choose to be without the gelim whispering in his ear, and if I quit, I'd never find out.

"Thanks, Orson. I'm really glad I met you."

Orson clapped me on the back. "Me too."

I turned visible, relieved that it hadn't been difficult, and went back out to the table. The others stopped talking when I returned, and I knew that meant they'd probably been talking about me. Blake wasn't the only person who needed to be better.

"I'm sorry I didn't believe you about Blake." I started

slowly, trying to gather my thoughts. "When he made jokes, I guess I just assumed that everyone was in on them." But the more I thought about the things Blake had said, the more I realized not everyone had been laughing. "I should've said something, told him to stop, but I didn't, and I'm sorry."

"Me too," Gordi said, and Evan added his apology as well.

I knew deep down that that wasn't who Blake was, because I'd seen what a great person he could be when we were alone, but that didn't change the hurt he'd caused others.

"Thanks," Jackson said, smiling, and just like that, everything was okay again.

After the bell rang, we were walking back to the main building, and I caught Sam looking at me.

"What?" I asked.

"We're going to save him," she said. "I promise."

"Do you think we can?" As soon as I said it, I realized how it sounded, and I added, "I'm not giving up. It's just, I couldn't even beat Blake in a race. How are we going to win against a literal monster?"

"Together," Sam said. "We're going to do it together."

## 34

ORSON FOUND PROOF that convinced even Sam that Conrad was the gelim, and she came over Saturday to share the news. "It's lucky I was at the school library late with Uncle Archie," she said. "Otherwise Orson would have had to wait until Monday to tell us."

"Spill it already." I was getting impatient.

Sam licked a bit of melted chocolate off her fingers and then snatched another chocolate chip cookie off the plate between us. Usually, Mom didn't let me eat in my room, but she'd made an exception for Sam. "Orson followed Conrad after school Friday. Every day this week, Conrad's gotten on the bus, but Friday he hid in Mrs. Gallagher's classroom until the other teachers had gone home. You'll never guess where he went after that."

"The clergy house," I said.

Sam's excited smile turned into a frown. "Did Orson already tell you?"

I shook my head. "But if Conrad's the gelim, and the clergy house is its nest, then it makes sense it's where he'd go. How long was he in there?"

"Don't know. Orson used the walkie in the hopes one of us was still there, and I think I surprised him when I answered. Anyway, he said he was going to keep watching over the weekend."

I didn't know what to say.

"You were right, Hector," Sam continued. "Conrad is the reason boys have been disappearing for seventy years, he's the reason Blake is acting so cruel toward you, and he's the reason Orson is stuck on the other side. And once we confront him, this could all be over."

"It's weird. When I first turned invisible, I thought it would be the coolest thing ever, like I was a superhero or something. But I'm not even turning invisible. I'm just going to the weird place lost socks wind up."

Sam looked different out of her school uniform, more relaxed. She leaned against the side of Jason's bed with her legs stretched out in front of her. "It's still pretty cool. Think about it. You're shifting over to an entirely different world."

"Yeah. A world with monsters."

"One monster," Sam said, but then added, "That we know of."

"It could've been me stuck like Orson." I looked up and

caught Sam's eye. "That's what the gelim does, right? It singles out boys no one will miss. I was invisible long before that day in the church."

Sam shook her head. "I don't think the gelim chose you."

I cocked my head to the side. "What do you mean?"

"I've been thinking about it, and the other boys disappeared about every five years, right?" Sam dragged over the backpack she'd brought with her and dug out a stack of folders. "You're right that the gelim bullies boys who are likely to slip through the cracks to the other side and then traps them there to feed off their fear. But it usually takes five years before it has to find another."

The way Sam talked about it made me feel even worse for Orson. He hadn't just been living there alone for three years—every day had been a fight for his life. And it was a fight he could never win, because even by surviving, he was giving the gelim exactly what it wanted.

"But it hasn't been five years since Orson disappeared," Sam went on. "I think your ability to travel back and forth surprised the gelim, and I'm pretty sure *that's* why it came after you, both by trying to lure you into the clergy house and by turning Blake against you. I don't think the gelim came after you because you're weak, but because something about you scared it."

I wanted to believe that, but the monster sure hadn't seemed scared of me. The last two times I'd seen it, I'd been the one doing all the running and screaming. But I had a feeling it was pointless to argue with Sam about it. Besides,

I had another question for her. "What if we rescue Orson and convince Conrad to leave, but Blake's still mean?"

Sam bit her bottom lip. "It's a possibility."

I was thinking about what Orson had said: that Blake had been a bully *before* he'd started hanging out with Conrad. "What if I don't want to save him?"

"You do," Sam said. "But even if you didn't, helping people doesn't mean only helping the people we like. Everyone deserves a chance to make amends. And if Blake is the person you believe he is, then you have to trust that he'll do the right thing."

Sam and I spent the rest of the afternoon working out exactly how we were going to get Conrad Eldridge alone and what we were going to say. Even though he was a monster, I didn't want to hurt him. I hoped we'd be able to convince him to let Orson go and leave St. Lawrence's. Sam didn't seem quite as optimistic.

After Sam left, I was in my room reading when Jason came in. He sat on the edge of his bed. I tried to ignore him, but I could feel his eyes on me. When I couldn't take it anymore, I looked over the top of my book and said, "What?"

Jason shook his head. "Nothing. Forget it." But then he didn't leave.

I shut my book and sat up. "What, Jason?"

"I overheard you and your friend talking about Conrad."

"What did you hear?" I asked cautiously.

"You should keep away from him. He's . . . there's something not right about him."

I thought back to how Jason had stood up for me when Blake cornered me by the library. "Why do you care? You don't even like me."

"But I like having a little brother."

That came as a surprise. "Really?"

Jason pursed his lips. "Just because I laugh at you for falling doesn't mean I won't punch the teeth out of anyone who pushes you down."

"Oh."

"Just stop messing with Conrad, okay? That guy gives me the creeps, and I really don't want to have to fight him."

"Thanks, I think." I didn't want any of us to have to fight Conrad Eldridge, but Jason's willingness to do it made me think he wasn't as bad as I thought. And if there was good in Jason, then maybe there was still hope for Blake.

## 35

**THE PLAN TO** trap and speak to Conrad was simple. If it worked. Lunch seemed like the best time to carry it off, since most of the teachers and students would be in the cafeteria. Sam slipped a note into Conrad's gym locker claiming I knew his secret and to meet me in the upstairs restroom during lunch. Then I hid in the stall and waited. Part of me hoped Conrad showed. Part of me prayed he wouldn't.

"I still don't think this is going to work," Orson said over the walkie-talkie. "You can't just ask the monster who's been terrorizing me and feeding off my fear for three years to please stop and expect it to agree."

I sighed and shifted position to ease a cramp in my left leg. "Maybe, but we don't know if we can hurt the gelim, and at least this way we have a chance of avoiding a fight we'd probably lose."

Before Orson could respond, the door opened. I peeked through the gap in the stall, but the angle was wrong, and I couldn't see who had entered.

"Well? I'm here." Conrad's voice sounded like sandpaper scraping against metal.

This was it. I slid back the bolt, opened the stall door, and turned out to face Conrad. The problem was that he didn't look like a monster. He had buzzed brown hair, a small upturned nose, and freckles across his cheeks. He reminded me of a harmless NPC from a video game. Maybe in another universe, Conrad and I could have been friends. Probably not in this one, though.

Conrad folded his arms over his chest. Even though he didn't know why we'd summoned him, he wore a smug grin. The overhead fluorescent lights were bright enough to throw faint shadows. Conrad didn't have one.

"Well?" Conrad said. "What's the big secret you think you know?"

Sam slipped into the restroom behind Conrad and locked the door. She caught my eye and nodded. That was the sign that we were alone and the restroom was secure. Conrad was trapped in the restroom with us so we could talk, though maybe it was more accurate to say that *we* were trapped in the restroom with *him*.

Conrad glanced over his shoulder at Sam. "No girls allowed."

"How—" Sam started, but I was already asking a different question.

"Does the name Orson Wellington mean anything to you?"

"Are you referring to the terrified little boy still hiding in the stall?" Conrad looked past me. "I can see your trembling legs, four-eyes. Why don't you come out?"

"You can see him?" I said.

"Uh, what do I do?" Orson's voice came through the walkie-talkie in my back pocket.

Conrad knew Sam was a girl, he could see Orson, and he didn't have a shadow. That pretty much confirmed he was the gelim. Now we just had to convince him to free Orson and leave Blake alone. "We know you've been making Blake act like a bully. We know you don't belong at this school. We know you're really the gelim, and that you've been making boys disappear from St. Lawrence's for seventy years."

Conrad tipped back his head and laughed, but the sound was hollow, soulless, devoid of joy. "You've got it all wrong about Blake, Hector. I merely cradle the embers and nurture the flames. Starting fires is *your* job."

Conrad's words slithered into my ears and wrapped themselves around my brain, cutting off my ability to speak. Maybe Conrad was right and *I* was the reason Blake had turned into a bully. I'd ignored it when he made jokes about other boys, I'd set him off asking him to be my boyfriend, and then I'd made it worse by destroying his science project. Maybe Blake was acting the way he did not because of what Conrad said to him, but because of what I'd lacked the courage to say. Maybe everything that had happened was *my* fault.

"Don't let him get in your head, Hector," Orson said through the walkie. "The gelim twists the truth."

As I hesitated, unsure what to say, Sam stepped up, her clear voice cutting through the haze in my mind. "What are you? What do you want?"

"I've had many names, but much like the refuse that spills from your world to mine, my true name has been lost." Conrad turned to Orson. "One of your predecessors named me gelim. It's incorrect but not inaccurate."

"You're a monster by *any* name!" Orson responded.

Conrad tsked and spread his hands. "Is a spider a monster because it eats flies? Is a lion a monster for feasting on gazelles?" Conrad returned his attention to me. "Are humans monsters for gorging on all the plants and animals of this world? Devouring everything in your path until there's nothing left?"

"Can we come to a compromise?" I asked. "We just want you to let Orson go and stop whatever you're doing to Blake."

Conrad tilted his head to the side. "Is that all? And what would you have me do, then?"

"I—"

"Should I leave my home? Travel to another school, maybe? Build a new nest? Cultivate a new crop of children willing to torment their peers? Tip the most vulnerable among them over the edge into my sticky web from which there is no escape and feed on them until nothing but a husk remains? You would be satisfied with our transaction as long as you don't have to know the names or faces of those upon which I dine?" Conrad looked at each of us in turn. "Who's truly the monster here?"

The gelim was right. We couldn't let it remain at St. Lawrence's, but we couldn't allow it to leave, either. We couldn't trade Orson and Blake for some other kids just because we didn't know them.

"Orson . . ."

His voice came through the walkie. "I know, Hector."

"Sam?"

Sam clenched her jaw and nodded. We'd each come to the same conclusion. There was no way to reason with the gelim. There was no deal we could reach. We couldn't negotiate with a monster.

"Ah," said Conrad. "So we've come to violence at last. You humans always resort to bloodshed. It's your way. You are as imprisoned by your nature as I am. Unlike you, however, I eat what I hunt."

Sam stepped toward the gelim. "I've faced worse than you, and we *will* stop you."

Conrad's head whipped around, and he sauntered toward Sam, hands in his pockets. "You're a strange one, like him." Conrad motioned lazily at me. "Though differently strange. You both travel places you don't belong, but he cowers among the lost while you walk brazenly among wolves."

"Leave her alone," I said, clenching my fists.

Conrad circled back around and leaned forward to sniff me. "Your terror is delicious. Aromatic and sweet. You can't fight me forever, traveler. Soon you'll belong to me, and I will feast for years." He licked his lips slowly.

"You're not going to do anything," Sam said. "We're not going to let you hurt anyone else."

"What are you doing?" I hissed at Sam. Our plan, if talking to Conrad failed, was to let him leave and then re-group to figure out our next steps. We weren't equipped for the fight Sam seemed to be leading us toward.

"Uh, Sam? Hector?" Orson's voice sounded small through the walkie-talkie.

Conrad was smiling, his teeth gleaming. "You actually believe you've captured me, don't you? You imagine that *this* body is the gelim, that I have imprisoned myself in *this* weak sack of flesh."

"Something's really, really wrong over here," Orson said, louder.

But my eyes were fixed on Conrad. I couldn't speak; I couldn't look away.

"Of course you're the gelim," Sam said. "You don't have a shadow. We saw you go into the clergy house."

Conrad's eyes were wide, his skin feverish. "You've heard, I'm sure, of *Ophiocordyceps unilateralis*, the delightful fungus that infiltrates an ant's body and transforms it into a puppet?"

"Yes," Sam said at the same time as I whispered, "Gross."

"The fungus uses the ant to spread its spores to other ants, creating a colony. Some fungal colonies are capable of remaining connected over vast distances." Conrad's smile became a sinister grin.

Sam's face fell. "You're not the gelim."

"Correct."

"You're impersonating someone else at this school," Sam said, "and using Conrad like a walkie-talkie."

"Correct again. And I think *this* particular ant has out-lived his usefulness."

"Something's happening here!" Orson shouted.

Conrad's body shook with laughter. His skin began to sag and wither, turning the color of crispy burnt bacon.

"Uh, Hector? I think we better go." Sam tugged my sleeve, pulling me toward the door.

Over the walkie, Orson was babbling, "No. Not now! Please not now!"

"Hector?" Sam said.

Conrad exploded, sending me flying backward. I slammed into the side of the restroom stall and slid to the floor, dazed. His laughter chased me in a dizzying spiral as I tried to surface.

"Hector?" Sam was calling my name.

I attempted to stand, but my legs were too wobbly. Orson reached out a hand to steady me. "Orson?"

His eyes were bulging, his body trembling. "We have to run," he said. "Can you run?"

Was I invisible? When had *that* happened? Nothing made sense, and my head hurt like a tiny wrecking ball was smashing through my brain. "Sam?"

"We need to run, Hector!" Orson was pointing to where Conrad had stood. In his place was a mass of writhing tendrils, grasping vines that were growing, thickening into tentacles and snapping teeth.

Orson yanked my arm, dragging me toward the door. He fumbled with the lock.

"See you for supper, Hector Griggs!" The gelim's voice no longer sounded like Conrad's. It was raspier, higher. Vaguely familiar.

Tendrils reached for me, attempted to slither around my ankle. I screamed and kicked them away. "Hurry!"

Orson flung open the door, and we ran. When we reached the stairwell, the gelim's tentacles burst up from below. Sam, oblivious to what was happening, was calling my name, but I couldn't answer her because I was too busy fighting for my life.

I ran into the nearest classroom and climbed around the desks to get out the back door. The smaller tendrils were already as thick as my legs and were spilling out of the restroom.

"Come on!" I pulled Orson with me. We had one chance. We had to get to the stairs at the front of the building before the gelim. I ran as fast as I could, sprinting as if my life depended on it. We were going to make it. We were going to—

"Hector!"

Orson tripped and fell. A tentacle from the restroom curled around his calf and pulled him away from me. The gelim from the stairwell snaked out and wrapped around his arm.

"Hector!" Orson screamed.

Moving with decisive speed, the tentacles and tendrils wrapped Orson in a cocoon and dragged him into the stairwell.

There was nothing I could do. The gelim was too strong, there were too many tentacles, and I had no weapons to fight them with.

So I ran.

I cried and I ran, and I didn't stop running until I reached the church. I shut myself inside a confessional booth, drew my knees to my chest, and prayed to turn visible again.

Nothing happened.

I squeezed my eyes shut and focused my thoughts on turning visible, but it was like a hand was pressing against my chest. Like there was an anchor tied to my ankle. No. I was like a butterfly pinned to a board. Stuck.

We'd thought that we were so smart, that we were going to reason with the gelim, convince it to free Blake and Orson, and end the threat to the school, but instead the gelim had captured Orson and trapped me. We'd failed, and it had cost us everything.

# 36

I COULD HEAR Orson's screams. I didn't know if they were real or a memory, but either way, I was too scared to leave the confessional. Orson was gone, and it was my fault. Before Conrad had dissolved into a mass of tentacles, he'd said the gelim was hiding in the body of someone else at St. Lawrence's, and we had no idea who. The gelim said it had invaded Conrad the way that creepy fungus invaded ants, so even though Sam had said there were no school records for Conrad, the file might've been lost or he might've gone by a different name. It was impossible to guess how long ago the gelim might've forced Conrad to become its unwilling servant. Conrad might have been a bully, but he didn't deserve what the gelim had done to him. What the gelim had made him do.

I kept trying to turn visible, but it was no use. It was like I was caught on one of those inhumane glue traps awful people use to catch rats, and I was going to be stuck, suffering, until I died.

After a couple of hours, when I was relatively certain the gelim wasn't coming for me, I poked my head out of the confessional. The church was empty. I crept to the storage area where Orson had shown me his hiding spot. As I rounded the corner, I held my breath, hoping to find Orson sitting among the junk he'd collected, but he wasn't there. No one was. I sat on the floor and cried.

More hours passed. I'd missed lunch and it had to be close to dinnertime now, but I wasn't hungry. Instead of hunger, I felt a gnawing emptiness in my belly. It was like the memory of being hungry. I wasn't tired, either. My arms and legs were sore, and I was weary, but I knew if I closed my eyes, I would spend hours staring at the backs of my eyelids, waiting for rest that would never come.

Night fell. I wondered whether Mom and Pop were looking for me. Did they know I was missing? Did they even remember I existed? I thought about Sam. Had she forgotten me? Had she looked around the restroom after Orson and I had fled, confused about why she was there? I wondered where the gelim was holding Orson.

But I already knew the answer to the last question: the old clergy house.

If St. Lawrence's was the spider's web, then the clergy house was the web's center, and as much as I wanted to rescue Orson, going there would be like dressing myself with salt and pepper and marching straight into the gelim's open mouth.

I'd been hiding in the church for hours when I heard a noise outside. A song. Someone singing. I couldn't make out the words, but I followed the melody out to the main hall, where I stood on a pew and pressed my ear against a stained-glass window.

*Come out, Hector,* the song seemed to say. *You've nothing to fear. You've nowhere to run, to hide. You've no way to fight, and time is on my side.*

I clamped my hands over my ears, but now that I'd heard the song, I couldn't block it out. The words were bees, busy building a hive in my brain.

> *Savory, salty, sweet, delicious.*
> *Your fear will season many fine dishes.*
> *For years and years, your tears I'll sip,*
> *your pain I'll tend,*
> *your sorrow I'll borrow but never amend.*
> *Until you're used up, dried out and empty,*
> *your hollow bones no longer plenty.*
> *And on that night, at that final meal,*
> *my scrummy boy, you will finally kneel.*

I ran back to Orson's hiding place and wedged myself against the wall. I didn't know how Orson had survived for three years when I doubted I could make it through a single night.

I hugged my knees to my chest and waited for daylight.

# 37

I DASHED FROM the church to the library as soon as I thought it was safe, though I knew from experience that it was never truly safe. The door was open, and I slipped inside. Sam was in the music room, punishing the drums. Her eyes were shut and her face was screwed up tight with pain as her arms moved like a hurricane spinning off tornadoes.

"Sam! Sam! I can hardly hear myself think." Mr. Morhill marched into the music room and stood with his hip jutted out and his arms crossed.

Sam stopped drumming and looked up. She held the sticks like weapons. "This is *my* fault, Uncle Archie. Mine. I went along with the plan to talk to Conrad Eldridge, and now we've lost Orson *and* Hector." Tears welled in her eyes but didn't fall.

Of course Sam had told her uncle. I should have expected she would. What surprised me more was that they both remembered me. Maybe that was a good sign that all wasn't lost.

"Are you crying, Sam? How are tears helpful right now?"

"There's nothing wrong with crying—"

"I haven't said there is," Mr. Morhill said. "I only asked how it's useful at this moment."

"What do you want me to do?" Sam asked. "Conrad is gone, I don't know where the gelim is, and I can't reach Hector or Orson. What, exactly, should I be doing?"

Mr. Morhill's stance softened. "Your job, Samantha. The thing you've been trained to do."

"How? I can't cross over the way Hector can."

"No, but there are, perhaps, other ways to sort this monster. I can assure you, though, that you won't discover them moping in here playing the drums."

Sam scoffed. "Easy for you to say."

Mr. Morhill paused. "I have faith in you, Samantha. So does Kairos." He nodded at her once before leaving.

Her job? Kairos? I had no idea what Sam and Mr. Morhill were talking about, but I was beginning to suspect Mr. Morhill was more than a librarian and that Sam was more than a student. I wondered if she was even really his niece.

Sam set the drumsticks aside and pulled out a walkie-talkie. She turned it on and held it close. "Hector? Are you there? Can you hear me? I'm in the library if you're in range."

I whipped the walkie-talkie out of my back pocket. I'd held on to it like a security blanket since our confrontation with Conrad.

"Hector, if you can hear me, talk to me, okay? I know things are bad, but I can help you. We can solve this. Together."

But what was the point? We couldn't talk to the gelim. We'd lost Orson trying to reason with it, and now I was lost too. That left us no choice but to fight, but we'd need an army to have a chance at defeating the monster. I doubted Sam would let that stop her from trying, but I couldn't bear the thought of something happening to anyone else because of me.

I understood Orson better now. His loneliness. How desperate he'd been for someone to talk to but also scared of being the reason someone else ended up lost. I even understood how his desperation for friends had driven him to frame Blake for stealing Musser's bangle. I didn't blame Orson for my situation, but I wasn't going to let Sam meet the same fate.

"Hector? Come on. I know you can hear me. Please talk to me, and let's figure this out."

I couldn't save Orson from the gelim or prevent it from capturing me, but I could make sure Sam didn't wind up its prey. I set the walkie down by the piano and left.

# 38

## I WENT HOME.

I reasoned that if the gelim lived and hunted at St. Lawrence's, then I'd be safer at home than school. Since no one could see or hear me, and no one but Sam and Mr. Morhill remembered me, I had no choice but to walk. I'd done it once before—Pop had gotten stuck at work, and Mom was at an appointment, so Jason and I had walked the four and a half miles to our house. It hadn't been so bad walking the distance with Jason, but it felt like it took forever alone.

I jumped every time I heard a strange sound. Since the gelim existed, it seemed likely that other monsters lived in this strange world where lost things wound up. I tried not to imagine what they might look like, but my mind conjured beasts with fangs and claws and scales and slimy underbellies. Monsters that fed on pain and fear and on invisible boys.

The gelim's song played in my head, stuck on a loop like one of Pop's old records.

To pass the time, I thought about Sam's conversation with Mr. Morhill. He'd said finding me was her job and had mentioned a strange name. *Kairos*. It sounded Greek, but I didn't know for sure. Sam was clearly more than she seemed, and I was beginning to think that it wasn't a coincidence she'd shown up at St. Lawrence's when she had. Maybe Mr. Morhill's arrival hadn't been chance either. Not that it mattered. Neither of them could help me. If they could, they would've done it already. I was stuck. Invisible. Forgotten. Like an old toy, left to gather dust.

My mom was the only person around when I finally made it home. She was busy working in her office. I sat down on the floor and watched her for a while. Even though she couldn't see me, I wanted to hear the sound of her voice.

"Please help me, Mom. Please just see me. Remember me. It's Hector, your son."

Mom typed and clicked and hummed to herself and never once looked up.

I wandered through the house. My bed and my belongings were still in my room. I wondered what would happen to them now that everyone had forgotten me. Would they eventually wind up in this lost place with me? Did Mom and Pop even see them or did their eyes slide past them? I went into Lee's room to poke around, since he never let anyone in, and was disappointed. It was messy, there were clothes and towels on the floor, and it smelled, but there was nothing interesting hidden there. I did find an old graphic novel that had slipped through the cracks, and I crawled with it onto my bed and spent the rest of the afternoon reading old books I thought I'd lost.

This wasn't so bad. In some ways, it wasn't much different from normal. Ever since Mom and Pop got married, I'd been a different kind of invisible. At least now I wouldn't have to endure dead legs or being forced to sit through Jason's baseball games. I could handle my new circumstances.

But my resolve crumbled at dinnertime.

Pop came home, and Mom began cooking. She was making fried chicken, macaroni and cheese, mustard greens, and biscuits. All the things I loved. I sat at the counter and watched her hum while she battered and fried the chicken. While she rolled and folded the dough. She smacked Lee's hand with a wooden spoon when he came by and tried to steal a piece of cheese, but she was smiling when she did it.

Jason and Lee played video games together. Pop set the table. Four plates, four sets of silverware, four glasses.

They didn't miss me. They were happy without me. The evidence of me was all around them—I was in the pictures on the walls, my books sat on the counter, my last math test was stuck to the fridge—but they couldn't see it. They couldn't see me. They'd filtered me out of the family and didn't notice I was missing.

"I'm right here!" I screamed as Mom called everyone to dinner. "Please just say my name! Hector! Your son! I'm here! Please just hear me! See me! Something!"

But they didn't. None of them did. I wasn't even a ghost. I was nothing at all.

"Mom, please?"

Now I understood why Orson had returned to St. Lawrence's. I couldn't imagine staying in the house I'd once lived in but never being seen. It would be a constant reminder that I was lost and unlikely to ever be found.

I ran out of the house and down the street. It was only when I was at the end of the road that I realized it was too late to return to school. I didn't know what might be lurking in the dark, waiting to make a meal of me. But I couldn't go home, either. I couldn't bear to spend a single second more in a house that didn't remember me.

Out of good options, I chose the least bad one and walked to Blake's house instead.

I stood at the scene of the crime. The last time I'd been in Blake's backyard, I'd been so angry I couldn't see straight. I'd held in my hand a lighter I'd borrowed from Pop's workbench in the garage. Blake and his moms had been out for the day. I knew what I was doing was wrong, but that word echoed in my head over and over. The name he'd called me that began with an *f* but wasn't *freak*. The name no one should ever call another person under any circumstances. With a flick of my thumb, I ignited the lighter and held the flame to the corner of the diorama.

The papier-mâché caught fire faster than I'd expected. I watched for a couple of seconds as the plastic dinosaurs melted and the volcano burned. Then I got scared of what

I'd done. The fire was spreading too quickly. I unspooled the hose, turned on the water, and put out the fire. Not soon enough to salvage Blake's project, though. It was irreparably ruined.

I wondered what Blake had said when he'd come home and seen his diorama—the project he'd spent hours creating—torched and waterlogged. I wondered if he'd cried or if he'd taken an express bus to anger.

I'd planned to throw the lighter away afterward to hide the evidence of what I'd done, but somewhere between Blake's house and mine, I'd lost it.

I peeked through the windows. Blake's moms were sitting together on the couch watching a movie. Dinner was done; the dishes were washed and put away. I didn't see Blake anywhere. Quietly, I opened the back door and slipped inside. I knew the Nesbitt house as well as my own.

"Hi, Mrs. Nesbitt. Mrs. N.," I said, as if this were a normal evening and they could hear me. I imagined them waving without looking, Mrs. Nesbitt telling me Blake was upstairs in his room.

I climbed the stairs. Blake was sitting on the floor playing the *Final Fantasy VII* remake. He loved the *Final Fantasy* games, though *VII* and *XV* were his favorites. He'd beaten both of them more times than I could count. I sat on the edge of his bed to watch for a while. I wasn't very good at video games—I could survive on easy mode—but Blake had serious skills. His fingers moved so fast I could barely follow them. The only time he ever slowed down was when we played two-player games together. He never complained about having to wait for me or that I was holding him back.

"I'm so sorry, Blake," I said. "I never should've set your science project on fire. I know I've said it before, but this time I really mean it. I was wrong."

My voice caught in my throat. I had to stop and take a breath before I could continue. "But you were wrong too. All those times you called me that name. I know words aren't supposed to hurt, but it did hurt because *you* were the one saying it."

Blake shook his head. He stuck his finger in his ear and wiggled it around.

I sat on the floor and tried to imagine everything was like it used to be. "I never had a best friend before you, Blake. I had friends at my old school, but I couldn't talk to them like I talked to you. There's no one in the whole world I like hanging out with more than you. That's why I wanted you to be my boyfriend. But even if you didn't want that, I never wanted to stop being your best friend."

On-screen, Blake was climbing the pillar in the Sector 7 Slums, fighting Elite Riot Troopers, and taking more damage than usual. He kept shaking his head and digging his finger into his ear canal.

"I wish I could blame the things you said and did on Conrad Eldridge, but I've been sitting with the cupcakes— you'd probably like them if you got to know them—and they said you've always been a little mean. Even Evan and Gordi said it's true.

"Maybe I didn't see it because I was right there laughing with you, which makes me kind of a bully too, but I know you're not really like that. That if you knew you were hurting people's feelings, you'd stop. It got me thinking about how a joke is only funny if *everyone* is able to laugh, and how you'd feel bad if you knew not everyone was able to laugh at yours."

Blake paused the game and dropped his controller. He pressed his palms against his ears and curled his lip. He squeezed his eyes shut and grimaced.

"Blake? Are you okay? What's wrong?"

He couldn't hear me, of course. No one could. After a few seconds, Blake shook off whatever had come over him and resumed playing.

"I miss you, Blake. I miss my best friend. I don't know if that's you anymore, but I really want it to be. I want everything to go back to the way it was before, when you could talk to me without looking like you wanted to punch me. When you didn't call me the terrible names people have called your moms." Tears welled in my eyes and rolled down my cheeks. "I'm so sorry, Blake. I'm sorry. I'm sorry. Please don't hate me anymore."

"Shut up."

His voice was so quiet, I thought I'd imagined it at first, but when I wiped my eyes, Blake was staring at me.

"Blake?"

"Shut up!" He dug his knuckles into his ears and groaned.

"Blake? What's wrong? Can you hear me?"

Thick, black tar bled from Blake's ears and dribbled down his neck.

"What *is* that?" I rose to run downstairs for help but stopped when I realized Blake's moms wouldn't hear me. I felt helpless, but I couldn't give up.

As I turned back to Blake, I remembered all the times Conrad Eldridge had whispered in his ear. The gelim had said it was like a fungus that had transformed Conrad into a mindless husk. What if this was how the monster had done it? Maybe every word the gelim had snuck into Blake had infected him. And maybe, somehow, I was the cure.

"You have to fight it!" I said. "You can beat it! You can do anything! I believe in you, Blake!"

Blake squirmed on the carpet, groaning, clawing at his ears like the sound of my voice was causing him pain. I didn't know if I was right about what was happening, but I had a feeling in my gut that I needed to keep talking.

"Remember last year when your mom Nora took us to the fair and we were trying to break Kyle McNeil's record for how many times we could ride the Gravitron? We got to seven and then you puked up funnel cake. I wanted to go home, but we only needed to ride once more to beat Kyle, and you refused to lose. That was way harder than this!"

"Shut up," Blake mumbled over and over. The inky syrup gushed from his ears, and I imagined it was every awful, hateful thing the gelim had filled Blake's head with. I hoped that was what it was. I'd never forgive myself if I'd hurt him.

"And remember when I had my piano recital in December, and I was scared I was going to mess up? You told me it didn't matter because everyone messes up and that's okay."

Blake was hardly moving anymore. The tar from his ears had slowed to a trickle.

"What about last year when Mr. Marshall made fun of Gordi for mispronouncing *viscount*, so you used the word every single time you could, always mispronouncing it the way Gordi had? You got everyone else saying it too, and then Mr. Marshall had to threaten detention to anyone who said it to make us stop."

I knelt beside Blake. "I don't think you're a bad person. I think you're a great person who did some bad things. Even after everything, I think you're my favorite person."

As soon as the words left my mouth, my body began to burn like someone had poured a bucket of magma over my head. I felt like one side of a piece of Velcro being torn from the other. It hurt worse than the time Lee had slapped a piece of duct tape to my arm and ripped it off. And then, as quickly as it had come on, the pain eased until it was nothing but a memory.

Blake slowly sat up, unsteady. He blinked, shook his head. He looked dazed. He looked right at me. "Hector?"

"You can see me?"

Blake threw his arms around my neck. "I'm so sorry, Hector. I'm so sorry for everything."

# 39

**I DIDN'T WANT** Blake to let go. Partly because it felt good to hug him after the last few weeks of him hating me, and partly because I was afraid that if he did, I might disappear again. But, eventually, Blake released his hold on me and sat back.

Thankfully, I remained visible.

"I don't understand what's going on," Blake said. "How did you get here? You weren't here before, right? Except I thought I heard your voice. I'm so confused."

I wasn't sure where to begin, so I tried to explain everything that had happened, though there were still parts I didn't understand.

"So, Conrad was this gelim thing?" Blake said. "And it was whispering in my ear, telling me to do bad stuff?"

I nodded. "Conrad was more like a puppet being controlled by the gelim."

"And you think it was trying to control me, too?" Blake looked at where I'd seen the puddle of gluey tar coming out of his ears. I couldn't see the stain anymore, but I figured I'd be able to if I turned invisible. Not that I was willing to try. The pain I'd felt must have been caused by me tearing free from the gelim's trap. I wasn't daring enough to test whether my freedom was permanent.

"Yeah."

Blake leaned against his bed and raked his hands through his hair. He had a set of beanbags he practiced juggling with, and he grabbed one and tossed it hand to hand as he worked through what I'd told him. "I still can't believe you can turn invisible. You're like a super specter or something."

"I knew you'd come up with a better superhero name than I could." I told him some of my ideas, and we both laughed for a while.

Then Blake was quiet. He held on to the beanbag and stared at the carpet. When he finally looked up again, he had tears in his eyes. "I didn't mean those things I said to you, Hector."

"I know," I said. "It was Conrad—"

Blake shook his head, cutting me off before I could finish. "No, I mean, yeah. The last couple of weeks are kind of a blur. I mostly just remember being angry all the time. Everything else is like trying to remember a dream."

"See, it's not your fault."

"I'm still sorry, but I was talking about before Conrad.

No one made me call you that name. I knew it was wrong the second I said it."

"So why did you?"

Blake sniffled. He wiped his eyes with his sleeve. "You're the best friend I've ever had, Hector. If I had a brother, I'd want him to be just like you." He paused like he was trying to figure out what to say next. "When you asked me to be your boyfriend, I got scared."

"Of what?"

"That if I said no, you wouldn't want to be my friend anymore."

"That's silly!" I said.

"It happened so fast," Blake said. "You surprised me when you asked, and my first thought was that if I didn't want to be your boyfriend, you'd find someone to replace me, and that made me so mad. Then I wished I could feel about you the way you felt about me, which made me wonder if there was something wrong with me. And then all those feelings got tangled up like when you're trying to beat a boss at the end of a level and you're doing everything right but still getting killed."

I nodded along, because I'd been killed by a *lot* of bosses at the end of a lot of levels.

"It all made sense to me in the moment. I was mad at myself for not liking you back, I was mad at you for springing it on me, and I was scared you were going to stop being my friend." Blake hung his head. "So I called you the name I knew would hurt you the most."

"It did," I said. "Hurt, I mean."

"I know," Blake said quietly. "And then, once I said it, I felt like I couldn't take it back, which made me even angrier."

"I've got the bruises to prove it." I tried to make it a joke, but the guilt in Blake's eyes silenced my laughter.

"The next day at school is when Conrad first talked to me. I don't know why I listened. If I'd just told him to go away and apologized to you, none of this would have happened." He wiped his nose with the back of his hand. "It was just easier to make everything that had happened *your* fault, and that way I didn't have to feel ashamed about what I'd called you. My moms would be so disappointed in me if they found out."

"The gelim used your anger to get in your head, I bet. It saw an opportunity and sent Conrad to poison your thoughts and turn you against me." I nudged Blake with my sneaker. "But it's okay. I forgive you."

"You shouldn't."

"What?" I said. "Why?"

Blake looked miserable. His eyes were puffy and his cheeks were red. "Because even if I don't remember everything I did or said, Conrad or the gelim or whatever it was couldn't have made me feel things that weren't already inside me. I'm not a good person, Hector."

I thought back to what Sam had said and what my mom had told me. "We all have bad in us. You called me names; I set your science project on fire. I'm not exactly innocent."

That made Blake laugh a little, and then hiccup. "Aren't you scared I'll call you names again?"

"Of course I am, but I think that's a good thing."

"How?"

"Because if I wasn't scared, it would mean I didn't care, and I don't want to not care about you, Blake. You're my best friend. Just promise, next time you get upset or angry about something I've done, you'll talk to me."

"I promise." Blake threw his arms around me again and hugged me so tightly I could barely breathe. "And I'm gonna make it up to you. I'm going to be the best friend you've ever had. I won't let anyone or anything hurt you."

I snorted. "You might not say that if you'd seen the gelim."

"I'd fight ten gelims for you." He let go of me and sat back. "Maybe we could tell it a joke. Do you think gelims like jokes? Because I've got some good ones."

Blake's bedroom door swung open, and Mrs. Nesbitt walked in. "Oh, Hector, you *are* here. I don't remember you coming in."

I was practically beaming because she could see me.

"That's because he was invisible before," Blake said.

"Blake!" I said.

Mrs. Nesbitt only laughed. "Well, your mom called looking for you, so you'd better go home. I'll let her know you're on your way."

I didn't want to leave Blake now that I'd gotten him back, but I wanted to see my mom again, and *be seen* by her.

"Meet me at the library tomorrow morning before school?" I said.

"You can count on me."

Mom was waiting for me in the kitchen when I got home. I expected her to be mad, but she wrapped me in a hug I never wanted to end. When she finally let go, I said, "What was that for?"

She brushed my hair off my forehead and smiled. "No reason. But all day, I've felt like there was something I'd forgotten."

Even though my mom hadn't remembered me while I was lost, maybe it was impossible for her to forget me entirely. Maybe some small, quiet part of her had known all along that I was missing. If that was true, then there was still hope for Orson.

## 40

SAM RAN ACROSS the library and nearly bowled me over. Mr. Morhill stood behind the circulation desk, watching with a sly smile on his face like he'd expected me to stroll through the door. "You're back!" Sam said. "How? When? *How?*" Before I could answer Sam's questions, Blake walked into the library. He looked around and smiled when he spotted me.

"What's *he* doing here?" Sam squared her shoulders and stood up straight.

I held up my hands to stop her from doing anything rash. "It's okay! He's all right! We're best friends again!"

Sam craned her neck, eyeing Blake skeptically. "Are you sure? This could be a trap."

"It's not," I said. "Come on. I'll tell you everything."

Sam paused before walking to the music room. Blake tapped me on the shoulder and whispered, "You were right.

She really is a girl." I suspected I'd broken Sam's illusion when I'd explained to Blake she was a girl the night before, but I didn't know for sure. Sam tended to avoid my questions when I asked about it.

Blake and I followed Sam into the music room, and I quickly told her everything that had happened after Conrad had trapped me in the place where lost things went. Even after my explanation, Sam didn't trust Blake, but she at least stopped glaring at him like she was working out a way to feed him to the gelim.

I had a lot of questions—like why she'd been able to remember me when everyone else had forgotten, how Blake had been able to hear me, and how I'd been able to become visible again—but the most important question on my mind was "How do we rescue Orson?"

"I think we have to fight the gelim head-on." Sam was holding the drumsticks, twirling one around her fingers while she paced the room. I wanted to talk to her about what I'd overheard—what "job" she was supposed to do, and who or what Kairos was—but with Orson's life in immediate danger, I needed to stay focused on him.

"That's impossible." I felt hopelessness creeping in. "It's too big, and we can't hurt it. I barely survived a single night alone hiding from the gelim. It could devour me in one bite."

Sam growled in frustration. "I know. I felt how powerful it was when we were talking to Conrad—ancient and strong and hungry."

"Can Kairos help?"

Sam looked at me like I'd barfed up frogs. "How do you know about them?"

"It doesn't matter. Can they help or not?"

"Hey," Blake said.

"Have you been spying on me?" I couldn't tell whether Sam was angry that I might have overheard something I shouldn't have or worried about how much I might have heard.

"Hector?" Blake said. "Sam?"

"I wasn't spying—"

"Then how do you know about Kairos?"

"If you can't hurt the monster in that weird lost place," Blake said, "why don't you bring it here?"

Sam and I stopped arguing and turned to face Blake. "What did you say?" Sam asked.

Blake had his hands in his pockets. He cleared his throat. "Bring it here. The monster, I mean. I don't know if it'd be any easier to fight it on this side, but at the very least you wouldn't have to fight it alone."

I shook my head. "I can't do it. I wouldn't even know how."

Sam wrinkled her nose. "What if it were possible, though?"

"It's not. Remember when I tried to bring Orson back with me? He slipped through my fingers."

"I've been thinking about the problem since then." That was news to me. Sam set her drumsticks aside and dug her notebook from her backpack. "I don't think people forget about the boys the gelim traps. I think the reason they become trapped is because the gelim makes the world forget them. We saw with Musser's bracelet that lost objects can return to our side, but the gelim makes sure that the boys who slip through the cracks can't come back by erasing them from memory."

I grimaced at the mention of Miss Musser's bangle, and mouthed *sorry* to Blake.

"So my theory," Sam went on, "is that if enough people remember Orson, you should be able to bring him home."

"But then how was *I* able to return? No one remembered me except you and Mr. Morhill." I cocked my head to the side. "How *did* you remember me?"

Sam ignored my second question. "You're different, Hector. Orson and the other boys slipped through the cracks and wound up in that other place, but *you* can travel there whenever you want. All you needed was an anchor on this side."

We both turned to look at Blake. "Me?" he said.

"When you freed Blake from the gelim's influence, you freed yourself." Sam shrugged as if it had been easy.

I considered Sam's theory, searching for holes, but couldn't find any that were obvious. "So you think if enough people remember Orson, I could rescue him from over there?"

Sam nodded. "And I think it would work to bring the gelim here too."

"Yeah!" Blake said. "There's no way that monster would fight the whole school!"

"Whoa, just slow down a second." I tried to get their attention, but Sam and Blake weren't listening to me.

"Hector could bring the monster over in the cafeteria during lunch." Blake was talking faster as he got more excited.

"That's perfect!" Sam said.

"Stop!" I yelled, and they finally did. "Neither of you saw the gelim. Even if I could make it visible, and even if we could hurt it, we could never defeat it."

"We don't have to," Sam said. "We only have to get it here and—"

"And Kairos will swoop in and finish the job?" I said, taking a wild guess. Sam was hiding things from me. Normally I wouldn't pry, but we were talking about putting our lives at risk.

"There's no time to explain everything," Sam said. "But I need you to trust me, okay?"

I caught her eye. "You'll tell me who or what Kairos is when this is over?"

"Promise."

"When should we do it?" Blake said.

"Today, if we can," Sam answered.

"Just to get this straight," I said, "the plan is for me to turn invisible, rescue Orson, lure the gelim to the cafeteria, and then make it visible in front of all the students?" The idea of returning to the place where lost things went soured my stomach.

Sam frowned. "I wish there were another way. But if it makes you feel better, now that you've broken free, I don't think the gelim can trap you again."

"Yay. Great."

Blake threw his arm around my shoulders. "You won't be alone, Hector. I'll go with you."

I shook my head. "I can't take anyone."

Sam cocked her head. "Have you tried with anyone other than me?"

"No, but—"

"I bet you could take Blake with you. I'd bet two Nutty Buddy bars on it."

"She sounds serious, Hector."

Sam's confidence was overwhelming. She believed what she was saying with her whole heart, and the only way I was going to prove her wrong was to try. I figured I might as well get it over with, so with Blake's arm still around me, I turned invisible.

"Did it work?" Blake let go of me and held his hand in front of his face. "Am I invisible? I can still see myself."

I looked for Blake's shadow, but it was gone. I'd done it! I'd made Blake invisible with me, and it hadn't even been difficult.

"Told you," Sam said. "Can you come back now?"

I grabbed Blake's arm, shut my eyes, and willed us back.

I was scared it wasn't going to work, but the force that had glued me in place last time was gone. Shifting from there to here was easier than ever.

"How?" I asked. "And how did you know?"

"I think you've always been able to take other people with you. Your ability just doesn't work on me, so we assumed it wouldn't work on anyone else."

I wondered if it didn't work on Sam for the same reason I'd always been able to see through her illusion and why she'd been able to remember me when everyone else had forgotten. But before I could ask, Blake said, "So we're doing this, right?"

"I can't force you to go, Hector," Sam said. "But I wouldn't ask you to do this if I didn't think you could."

I wished I believed in myself as much as Sam and Blake seemed to. But Orson had been running from the gelim for years, and it was my fault it had finally caught him. If there was even a tiny chance I could save him, I owed it to him to try.

— — — — — —

In order for our plan to work, we had to convince the other students at St. Lawrence's that Orson Wellington and the gelim were real. Sam volunteered to spread the story through the seventh-grade classes, and Blake and I could handle sixth grade, but for the story to really take root, we needed to get the eighth graders talking about Orson and the monster. The only student any of us knew who might be willing to help was the last person I wanted to ask.

Jason was sweaty from playing basketball when Blake and I found him after leaving Sam in the library.

"What do you want, pianist?"

"Can I talk to you?"

Jason rolled his eyes at his friends and walked over to where we were waiting. "What?"

"I need your help," I said. "I can't explain why, but I just need you to believe me."

Jason motioned at Blake. "I guess you're friends with *him* again."

"Yeah."

"Think you can trust him?" Jason sounded concerned. Almost brotherly.

I could feel Blake beside me itching to respond. He'd never gotten along with Jason. "We talked. Everything's okay now."

Jason glared at Blake. "He apologize?"

"I did," Blake said. "And it'll still never make up for how awful I was."

If Jason could get the eighth-grade boys talking about Orson and the gelim, the lower grades would follow. Our plan wouldn't work otherwise. "Please, Jason? I really need your help."

Jason eyed Blake one last time before turning back to

me. "Fine, tell me what you want, but don't come crying when he calls you names again."

The bell was going to ring soon, so I explained to Jason about the gelim and Orson Wellington as quickly as I could.

"Let me get this straight," Jason said. "You want me to tell my friends that there's an invisible monster in the school that steals bullied boys and feeds off their fear?"

"Basically, yes."

"And the monster *isn't* Mrs. Ford?"

The problem was that I wasn't sure whose skin the monster might be wearing. It *could* have been Mrs. Ford, but she seemed way too obvious. "Just tell them what I told you, and don't forget about Orson Wellington."

"Yeah," Jason said. "All right."

"Look, if you don't—" I stopped when I realized he'd agreed. "Wait, you'll do it?"

Jason shrugged. "Sure. I've heard weirder stories."

The bell rang and everyone began forming into lines.

Jason gave me a shove toward my class. "Whatever this is about, be careful, okay?"

"Thanks, Jason."

Jason wrinkled his nose. "Just don't hug me, okay? I'll punch you if you try."

# 41

BY FIFTH-PERIOD PE, everyone was whispering about Orson Wellington and the gelim. The story spread through the school faster than head lice and took on a life of its own. Students were claiming they'd known Orson, while others were saying they'd seen the gelim. I didn't know how many people actually believed that Orson and the monster were real, but they were talking about them, and that was what mattered. I hoped it would be enough.

I was changing into my gym clothes when Gordi and Evan cornered me in the locker room.

"Hey," Gordi said, "so you're friends with Blake again?"

Evan kept looking over his shoulder to where Blake was changing on the other side of the room.

I nodded.

"Even after the stuff he said?" Gordi bit the end of his thumbnail nervously. "The things he said to your face were nothing compared to what he said when you weren't around."

When I'd forgiven Blake, I'd forgiven him for everything, but I was still glad I didn't know the awful things he'd said about me behind my back. "He only said those things because of Conrad."

Evan's eyebrows dipped to form a V, and he was looking at me like I'd spoken Hylian.

"Who's Conrad?" Gordi said.

No one seemed to remember Conrad Eldridge now that he'd disappeared. I didn't know how to explain to them that he had been a tool used by the gelim to poison Blake. "Forget it. The point is, Blake and I talked. He apologized, and everything's better."

Gordi frowned. "He didn't apologize to me."

I hadn't thought about that. Blake was my best friend again, but that didn't magically cancel out anything he might have said or done to the other boys. I had no right to expect them to forgive him. "You don't have to be friends with him if you don't want, but maybe you could talk to him. He hasn't been himself lately, and I bet he'll listen if you tell him how you feel."

Evan and Gordi both looked skeptical, and I couldn't blame them. I hoped they would give Blake a chance, but it had to be their choice.

"Hector, my office. The rest of you, head outside and divide into teams for flag football." Coach Barbary's voice cut through the noise in the locker room.

Unsure why Coach wanted to talk to me, I slunk to his office. On the wall hung the whiteboard on which he'd written our class's rankings from the events of the week before. I stood dead last. Coach was sitting with his hands folded on his desk.

"Did you know I was a student here when I was your age?" Coach said. "Kindergarten through eighth grade. Musser was a young teacher back then, and we had Principal Mitchell instead of Principal O'Shea, but Miss DeVore was still working in the office, looking the same as she does now."

It was weird trying to imagine Coach being my age or Miss Musser being young.

"I had a best friend. Gideon Lane. We used to sit together during lunch and read comic books. We weren't very popular, but it didn't matter, because we had each other."

"Are you still friends with him?" I asked.

Coach glanced down. "Gideon disappeared during seventh grade."

I sat up and paid closer attention to Coach's story.

"The strangest part was that everyone seemed to forget about him afterward, even his parents. But I couldn't forget." Coach looked up. He was smiling. "No matter how bad I was feeling, Gideon would do *anything* to make me laugh."

"He sounds like a good friend, Coach."

"The very best." Coach Barbary looked different. Less

intimidating. "But we'd been fighting before he disappeared. We hadn't spoken to each other in a couple of weeks. I was angry at him for something silly. Maybe if we hadn't quit talking, he wouldn't have vanished."

A thought occurred to me. "Is that why you forced me and Blake to run laps together?"

Coach Barbary offered up a half shrug. "I just think you boys are better off when you're helping each other instead of tearing each other down, even if all you're doing is helping each other be pains in my butt."

"Can I ask a question, sir?" When Coach motioned I could, I said, "Why'd you make us compete last week?"

"To show you boys that everyone's good at something. Even you."

"But I came in last in nearly every event."

Coach glanced over his shoulder at the board and grunted. "Only because you quit when you fell down. So, next time you fall, I expect you to get up and keep running."

"Aren't there times it's okay to quit?" I asked. "Like if you get hurt or something?"

"Of course." Coach nodded gently. "Taking care of your body *and* mind are important, and it's okay to admit you need a break or ask for help. But that's not the same as giving up when things get tough. As long as you try your hardest and stay true to yourself, you'll never lose. Understand?"

"Yes, sir."

Coach nodded. "Good. And one more thing." He tossed a small shiny object at me. I caught it and turned it over in my hand. Coach Barbary had given me a key. I returned a questioning look and he said, "Never know when it might come in handy."

# 42

SAM, BLAKE, AND I met in the upstairs restroom when the bell rang releasing us for lunch. While the rest of the students were walking across the parking lot to the cafeteria, we made our final preparations to confront the gelim and rescue Orson.

"You only have forty-five minutes before the end of lunch," Sam said for what felt like the tenth time.

"Got it."

"And don't try to fight the gelim. Just get to the clergy house, rescue Orson, and lure the monster to the cafeteria."

Blake spoke up. "How do we get the gelim to the cafeteria?"

"I think that'll be the easiest part of the plan." Sam shoved her hands in her pockets. "What would you do if someone tried to steal *your* lunch?"

"Probably let them have it," I said.

Blake snorted. "I doubt the gelim's that generous."

Sam handed me a new walkie-talkie. "I'll keep mine on in case you need me." Then she threw her arms around my neck. "Good luck!"

I looked at Blake after Sam let go of me and ducked into the stall to hide. "You ready?"

"Always."

My whole body was trembling. The thought of turning invisible again and facing the gelim made me want to throw up. All I'd been able to do last time was run and hide in the church. How was I going to rescue Orson when I'd barely managed to save myself?

Blake took my hand and squeezed. "Let's go save your friend, okay?"

I nodded, unable to speak, and became invisible.

"This is so weird!" Blake rushed to the mirror to admire his lack of reflection.

As much as I wanted to let Blake enjoy this, we didn't have time to fool around. "We should go." Blake looked over his shoulder at me and then followed me out the door.

"So, we're not actually invisible, are we?" Blake said as we walked to the clergy house. It felt weird to be willingly heading to the monster's lair, but if Orson was still alive, I was certain that was where the gelim would be holding him.

"Not really."

"Then maybe you should call it something different?"

"Like what?"

Blake shrugged. "Shifting?"

"Maybe," I said. "But even if I'm not really invisible, it feels like I am. No one sees me, no one hears me, and everyone forgets about kids who get stuck here, though I guess that's the monster's doing."

"Oh." Blake was quiet for a moment. "How's it been, sitting with the cupcakes at lunch?"

"You shouldn't call them that," I said. "They're actually pretty great." It felt weird standing up to Blake, but I wished I'd done it sooner.

"I didn't mean—" Blake stopped. "You're right. I'm sorry. I guess the truth is I'm kind of jealous."

"Of what?"

"I used to think you wouldn't have any friends without me if something happened and we wound up at different schools, but it's the other way around, isn't it?"

"No—"

"Come on, Hector. It only took a couple of weeks for everyone to bail on me. I'm starting to think the only reason anyone hung out with me was because of you."

"But that was because of Conrad."

"It wasn't all Conrad." Blake stuffed his hands in his pockets.

I remembered how upset I'd been when the boys at lunch had shared their feelings about Blake. He was handling it better than I had. "It's just that sometimes you can be mean when you think you're being funny."

"Yeah, I know," Blake said. "But if people are laughing at someone else, then they're not laughing at me." He hung his head. "I've got a lot of people to apologize to."

I slung my arm around Blake's shoulders. "When this is all over, I'll introduce you to everyone. I think you'll like them once you get to know them." Gordi and Evan and Jackson had every right not to forgive Blake, but I hoped they would.

It was probably my imagination, but the sky seemed to grow darker as we approached the clergy house. I felt like it was watching us, looming, preparing to pounce. But it was only a building, and buildings weren't alive. The real danger lay inside.

Blake slowed as we crept around the side to the door the gelim had attempted to lure me through last time. "Does it make me a coward that I don't want to go in?"

"It makes you smart." I paused. "You don't have to do this. I can find Orson without you."

Blake smiled and shook off the fear that had settled over him. "I know you can, Hector, but you don't have to. We're in this together."

I smiled back, relieved Blake hadn't changed his mind. I took a deep breath and tried the door. The knob wouldn't turn. The gelim had attempted to lure me inside twice before, so I'd expected it to be unlocked.

"What do we do now?" Blake craned his neck, looking for another way in. "We could try to pry the shutters off one of these windows. Or we could look for a ladder. The windows on the second floor aren't covered."

I reached into my pocket and pulled out the key Coach Barbary had given me. *I wonder . . .* The key slid effortlessly into the lock and turned.

"Whoa." Blake's eyebrows shot up. "Where'd you get that?"

"Coach," I said.

"For real?"

I didn't understand it either. How had Coach Barbary known I would need to get into the clergy house? I promised myself that if I survived, I'd ask next time I saw him. "Come on." I opened the door and led Blake inside.

With the shutters covering the first-floor windows, there was barely any light to see by, but that might have been for the best. The floor was coated with a layer of grime, and sinewy cobwebs hung from the ceilings and corners. Mold and mildew streaked the wood-paneled walls, crawling over the surface like an infection. Even the air in the house felt hot and diseased. Lost and forgotten objects lay everywhere I looked. Eyeglasses, coffee mugs, three fountain pens, stacks of books, orphaned shoes, marbles, pencil cases, toy cars. The clergy house was like a tide pool, teeming with students' belongings that had slipped through the cracks of the real world. I found a baseball bat and grabbed it, curling my fingers around the grip.

Blake furrowed his brow. "I thought you couldn't touch stuff while you're invisible?"

I handed him the bat. "If it doesn't have a shadow, then it's real over here."

Blake pulled something from his pocket that turned out to be a penlight. He switched it on and swung the beam around. There were so many items without shadows piled precariously along the walls that I felt like they could crash down and bury us at any moment. "There could be some valuable stuff hiding in this junk."

The idea of digging through it turned my stomach, though. "Come on. We need to hurry."

Blake tried to return the bat, but I told him to hold on to it. He was better at baseball than me anyway.

The clergy house was much bigger on the inside than it seemed from the outside. We picked a doorway on the right side of the hallway and went in. The room, which might have been used as a sitting room when the clergy house was first built, was stuffed full of cardboard boxes and stacks of old yearbooks. They'd been stacked there for so long that they were solid to us, and we had to navigate around them like a maze to keep them from toppling over.

Blake yelped and stumbled into me.

"What?"

"Roaches, Hector. And I think they can see us."

I didn't like roaches either, but Blake was terrified of them. Especially palmetto bugs, which was just a fancy name for roaches that could fly. "Orson told me once he thought cockroaches could cross back and forth from here to there, which is why they're so good at staying alive."

"Great," Blake muttered. "Another reason to hate them."

I hurried him along, and we stumbled into the kitchen.

It looked like it had been abandoned in the middle of a meal. A table stood in the corner, still set with dust-covered dishes. Black mold spilled across the linoleum floor, and there were pimple-like eruptions along the wall that pulsed with a heartbeat and oozed gray mucus.

"I think we're going the right way."

"That's what scares me," Blake said.

On the corner of a dusty table sat a familiar plastic object. I drifted toward it and reached for it before Blake's voice stopped me. "What is that?"

I couldn't believe what I was seeing. Quietly I said, "It's the lighter I used to set your project on fire."

"Seriously?"

I nodded, not trusting myself to speak. It was definitely the same lighter. I recognized the gouges along the bottom edge from Pop using it to open bottles.

"How did it get here?" Blake asked.

"I thought I'd lost it after I . . ."

Blake put his hand on my shoulder. "It's okay. It's in the past, remember?"

I wished I could forgive myself as easily as Blake had. "The gelim must've found it and brought it here."

"Should we take it?"

My hand was still outstretched. "No," I said. "Leave it."

We crept through the kitchen, careful not to touch anything, but I swore we were being watched, our movements tracked by things that hid in the shadows but didn't have shadows themselves. The room beyond the kitchen was filled with ancient wooden desks, which blocked our path like brambles that we had to climb over to pass. On the way back to the hallway, I found a golf club with a heavy metal head. Pop had tried to teach me to play golf, but I'd barely managed to hit the ball even once. This time I'd be aiming at something much larger, though I didn't know if that was a good thing or not.

Sam's voice crackled through the walkie-talkie, causing me and Blake to jump. We yelped and then fell into each other, laughing through the fear.

"How's it going?" Sam asked.

"We're in the clergy house," I said. "It's creepy. We haven't found Orson yet."

"Hurry up. You're running low on time."

Sam wasn't wrong, but it was too dangerous to rush ahead. There was a possibility that the gelim was waiting for us, using Orson to lure us into a trap, and we had to be careful not to stumble into it. I slipped the radio back into my pocket and turned to Blake. "Which way?"

Blake looked around. "We should probably check every room just to be sure, but my gut is telling me to stay away from the upstairs, so that's probably where we should go."

I couldn't even look at the stairs without creepy-crawlies skittering across my skin. The black mold and the barnacles were thicker on the banisters, and the second floor seemed to suck in the light. As desperately as I didn't want to go up there, I knew Blake was right. "Come on."

I led the way up the stairs. My loafers squelched on the

steps like they were sticking in mud, and I had to lift my legs higher to pull them out.

Blake let out a nervous giggle. "This feels like a video game. You and me creeping through the enemy's lair to fight the big boss at the end of the level."

I couldn't help smiling. "Too bad I can't play this one on easy mode."

"Why are the walls moving?" Blake asked when we reached the landing. He turned on his penlight. Roaches scattered in every direction. Blake screamed and staggered backward, forgetting the stairs were behind him. He flailed his arms, accidentally flinging his penlight into the darkness below. I spun fast and grabbed his shirt to keep him from falling, but I had to drop my golf club and clutch the railing for balance. I managed to pull Blake back from the edge, but my hand sank into the banister, and slimy green tendrils curled around my fingers.

"Help!"

Blake slammed his bat into the railing, and it released me with a shriek. I cradled my hand to my chest. It felt burned and blistered but didn't look injured.

"Are you okay?" Blake asked.

I nodded, not trusting myself to speak.

"At least we know we're in the right place."

I kept my eye on the banister as I retrieved the golf club. "Come on."

We checked each room. Most of them were empty or filled with junk. Decades of accumulated stuff that had been sealed up, stored away, and forgotten. The boxes and trunks were overgrown with the strange barnacles, and Blake and I had to walk carefully to avoid the colonies of glistening black mold on the floor. Blake stopped and pointed at a thick puddle of the stuff. "Is that what came out of my ears?"

I nodded grimly.

Blake tried and failed to suppress a violent shiver.

When we finished exploring the last room, Blake turned to me. "What now?"

There was only one place we hadn't searched. "Attic?"

"I was hoping you wouldn't say that."

At the end of the landing on the second floor, there was a small opening in the ceiling. Blake knelt so I could climb onto his shoulders, and then he slowly stood, allowing me to reach the handle and pull down the expanding staircase. A burst of putrid air blasted from the hole, causing me to splutter and gag.

This was it. I was convinced that if Orson was still alive, we'd find him in the attic. As Blake moved toward the stairs, I stopped him.

"Whatever happens," I said, "you have to get Orson out of here."

Blake looked at me like I had roaches crawling out of my nose. "As if I'd leave you."

"I don't want you to, but we don't know what shape Orson is going to be in, and he might need your help more than I do."

Blake was shaking his head. "Hector—"

"Promise me," I said. "I can take care of myself, okay?"

Blake's shoulders slumped and he nodded. "Only if there's no other choice."

"Deal."

I held on tightly to my golf club and Blake gripped his bat. We both turned to face the attic and ascended the stairs.

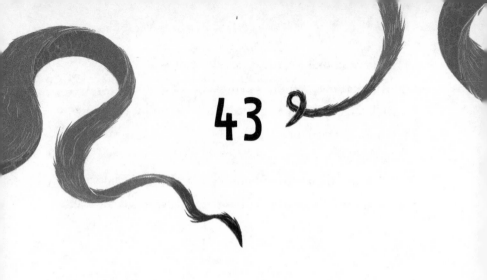

# 43

**THE BARNACLES WERE** thickest in the tight space of
the attic. They grew like blisters from the floor and walls
and ceiling. Overhead, the eruptions dripped gray mucus
that solidified into stalactites. Black mold clung to every
surface. It reminded me of a fruiting fungus that Miss
Musser had brought in to show the class once.

"Careful not to touch anything," I whispered.

"Don't have to tell me twice."

It was darkest in the attic. Blake had lost his penlight
when he'd nearly fallen down the stairs, so our only light
came from small windows at either end of the room, but
they were so caked with dirt and grime that they were
hardly better than nothing. The entire attic seemed to
breathe and squirm. Skittering noises ricocheted off the
walls cloaked in shadows, the sounds coming from everywhere all at once.

"Hector, look!" Blake pointed at a pair of loafers poking out of a pool of slime. "There's more over here."

As my eyes adjusted to the lack of light, I spied other objects trapped in the mold like bugs in amber. A textbook, a pair of glasses, a backpack. Something shiny caught my attention, and I used my golf club to fish it out. It was a stainless-steel dive watch. I used my pants to clean the slime off it and turned it over. On the back was engraved HAPPY BIRTHDAY, GIDEON!

"Do you think this stuff belonged to St. Lawrence's boys who disappeared?" Blake asked.

It did. Everything in the attic belonged to someone who'd been trapped by the gelim. This was more than a place where lost things wound up. It was a graveyard. I slipped the watch into my pocket. "Let's find Orson."

We pushed on slowly. It was difficult to see, and I worried we might walk past Orson without realizing it. I heard a groan from up ahead and moved toward the noise. I gripped my golf club tightly, preparing for the worst. Deep in the shadows, in the farthest corner of the attic from the door, we finally found Orson. He was glued to the floor, sitting up, his legs sprawled out in front of him. His entire body up to his chin was encased in thick slime and barnacles, and his face was wan and lifeless.

"We have to get him out of this!" I fell to my knees and tried to use the golf club to dig Orson free, but the blunt head couldn't break through the thick mucus.

Blake pulled a Swiss Army knife out of his pocket and

flipped open the small blade. "Thought this might come in handy." He stabbed the knife into the slime and cut through it cleanly.

The house shook. It screamed. Orson's eyes fluttered and he moaned.

"Keep going," I said.

As Blake sliced deeper, I sank my fingers into the openings he made, ignoring the ooze as it burned my hands. I grabbed hold of Orson's arm and pulled it loose. As Blake and I worked, I sensed things moving in the dark around us, toward us, but I remained focused on Orson. Blake was hacking through the slime as fast as he could, but it tried to seal shut almost as soon as he wounded it. Together, we managed to expose Orson's foot, but at the rate we were working, lunch would be over before we cut all the mold away.

Blake wiped sweat off his forehead with the back of his hand. "Let's try pulling him the rest of the way out."

With me holding Orson's wrist, and Blake his ankle, we struggled to free him, heaving with all our strength. The slime refused to let him go.

"This is the worst game of tug-of-war ever," I said through clenched teeth.

Orson opened his eyes and cried out. He fought against the mold *and* us, flailing wildly, unaware of what was happening, but Blake and I held tight, and with one final heave, we tore Orson out of his gooey prison.

The momentum sent the three of us tumbling backward, and we landed in a heap. Something wet tried to latch on to my arm, but I shook it off and scrambled out of its reach. "We have to get out of here."

Blake was on his feet first. A tendril loomed in front of us, dancing side to side like a cobra, blocking the path to the exit. Blake juked to the right, snatched the golf club I'd dropped, and swung for the fences. The tentacle screeched and recoiled warily.

"Orson?" I shook his shoulders to wake him. "Orson, can you hear me?"

"Hector?" His voice was froggy and weak.

"Yeah, buddy. It's me."

"You came?" His smile was fragile.

"Of course I did," I said. "We're friends, right?"

Orson's eyes rolled back, showing only the whites for a second. "I was so scared. Couldn't wake up from the nightmare."

"The gelim can't hurt you anymore." I slipped his arm around my shoulders. "Can you walk?"

Orson tried to stand, but his legs were wobbly and barely able to support him.

"Hector, we can't stay here." Blake was swinging away, knocking back tendrils as they grew from the puddles of black slime and attacked.

Orson took one step and stumbled, dragging us both to our knees. "Go without me."

"Like I'm leaving you now after I went through all this trouble to find you." I tried to force a laugh so he wouldn't know how terrified I was, but I nearly choked on it. "Blake, you're stronger. I need your help with Orson."

Blake handed me the golf club and took over supporting Orson. As soon as they were together, I made a decision I hoped they'd understand and wouldn't hate me for. "Get to the cafeteria and tell Sam I'm coming."

I hadn't had much time to consider what I was doing. I didn't think we stood a chance of escaping the house if we had to fight *and* carry Orson. If Sam, Blake, and I had done our job well that morning and everyone knew who Orson Wellington was, then it should have been possible for all three of us to escape by shifting back to the other side. But then we might lose the chance to lure the gelim to the cafeteria. That was when I remembered Miss Musser's bangle. Orson had described being able to push lost objects back to our world where they belonged, and nothing was more lost than us at that moment.

I knew that if I tried to explain my reasoning to Blake, he would argue, so I just did it. I shoved Orson and Blake from here to there with all my strength. From Blake's and Orson's points of view, the transition would be instantaneous. For them, the mold and slime and tentacles would vanish as they found themselves standing in a regular dusty old attic without me.

Blake's eyes widened when he realized what I'd done. "Hector! No! You can't do this! Hector!"

Orson looked around, blinking, like he couldn't believe he was finally home. *Thank you,* he mouthed.

Blake and Orson were still standing in the attic. I could see and hear them, but they were safe on the other side, where the house and the gelim couldn't hurt them.

But now I was alone.

Now that I didn't have to worry about supporting Orson, I dashed through the attic, swinging the golf club wildly to keep the slimy tendrils away. I dove down the stairs and raced to the first floor. Getting out of the house wasn't going to be difficult. The real problem would be convincing the gelim to show up and chase me to the cafeteria. Like Sam, I'd expected it would follow us because we had Orson, but with Orson gone, I needed a new idea, and I had one. It just wasn't a good idea. In fact, it was an exceptionally bad idea. But bad ideas were all I had left.

I ran back into the kitchen and grabbed the lighter.

# 44

**TO TELL THE TRUTH,** I'd learned my lesson about starting fires after I'd destroyed Blake's science project. Fire was dangerous, and I shouldn't have been messing around with it. I was glad when I'd lost that lighter and had promised myself I'd never do anything like that again. But so many boys had been lured to the clergy house and trapped in that attic. They'd spent their last days confused and terrified while the gelim fed on their fear. I couldn't bear to leave such an evil place standing. Orson had said we could bulldoze a building in this world and it wouldn't affect the building in the real world. I hoped he was right.

"Hey, gelim! I'm here!" I didn't have time to figure out what would burn the fastest—there were so many good candidates—so I went straight to the old curtains. As soon as I flicked the wheel that created the spark that brought the flame to life, the house shuddered. I wondered if the house was part of the gelim or if it was its own separate monster. I'd read about a forest of aspen trees in Utah that shared a single root system. Maybe the house and the gelim were connected that way.

I held the flame under the curtains. "Where are you?" I shouted. "I'm here! How'd your song go? You thought I would kneel, right? Think again!"

The house flinched from the fire and recoiled from the heat, but the gelim didn't appear. I lifted the lighter to the curtains. The thirsty fabric burst into flames. The house screamed, and it sounded like someone slamming down all the keys of a busted, out-of-tune piano. I raced across the hallway and lit the curtains in that room. It only took a few seconds, but the fire in the sitting room was already spreading across the wood paneling and the ceiling, advancing toward the cardboard boxes stacked throughout. The clergy house was a tinderbox, primed to burn.

Smoke filled the house. I headed for the front door to escape. I barely made it outside before a meaty tentacle wrapped around my chest and tried to wring me out like a wet towel.

"What have you done?" the shrill voice of the gelim screamed. It flung me through the air. As I hit the grass, more tentacles snaked out from around the side of the burning house to loom over me, the snapping teeth slavering for revenge.

I stood and brushed myself off, ignoring the pain pulsing from every bruise I'd suffered, and faced the gelim. Smoke poured from inside the house. "What's wrong? Lose your lunch? I guess if you're hungry, you'll have to catch *me!*"

Then I dashed toward the cafeteria as fast as I could, and I didn't look back.

Sam and I had used Google Maps to measure the distance between the clergy house and the cafeteria. I had to race across the PE field, hop the wooden fence, turn at the main school building, and then make it across the parking lot. It was almost three hundred meters total. Since fighting with Blake, I'd spent a lot of time running, so three hundred meters was nothing, but I'd never done it while an enraged, ravenous monster was chasing me.

My lungs were on fire, and I was sore from being thrown by the gelim, but with the wind in my hair and the sun on my face, I felt like I could fly. When I hit the low wood fence, I leapt over it, clearing it easily, and put on a burst of speed. I was going to do it. I was going to beat the gelim to the cafeteria, where Sam and everyone were waiting.

I reached the main building and arced toward the cafeteria. As I did, my sneaker caught the edge of a sprinkler head poking out of the grass. My ankle turned and gave out. I hit the sidewalk in a heap.

*No, no, no, no! Not now!*

The gelim made a croaking noise that sounded like a cruel imitation of laughter.

I was bleeding from new scrapes and old. I wanted to cry. But then I thought about what Coach Barbary had said. The only reason I'd lost my race to Blake was because

I'd quit. There were times when it was okay to fall back and retreat, times when the bravest act was admitting that winning wasn't worth the cost. My race with Blake hadn't been one of those times, and neither was my race with the gelim. Because this wasn't just about winning. It was about surviving. It was about making sure the gelim couldn't hurt me or anyone else ever again. And that was worth a little pain.

I pushed myself to my feet and carefully put weight on my injured ankle. It was sore, but I hadn't sprained or broken it. This was it, the last leg. Just one long sprint across the parking lot to the cafeteria. I could do this. I *had* to do this. Too many people were counting on me.

The gelim's tentacle lashed across the space where I'd been standing, smacking a palm tree, but I was already gone.

I ran. I ran faster than I'd ever run before. I ran faster than my fear, faster than my pain. Faster than the gelim. Instead of hearing the monster whisper that I was going to fail, I heard Blake shouting that I could do it, the cupcakes cheering me on, Sam saying she believed in me. Their voices, and my own, were louder than doubt. The cafeteria grew closer. I could feel the gelim behind me, even if I couldn't see either of us reflected in the cafeteria's glass doors. I sensed the monster gaining on me, but it wasn't quite fast enough to catch me. I was going to beat it. I was going to win.

I reached the doors, flung them open, and crossed that finish line. Sweat dripped from my hair and down my face.

I could barely breathe, but I yanked my walkie-talkie from my pocket and gasped, "I'm here."

I stood in the empty area at the front of the cafeteria while five hundred students finished their lunches. I backed away from the doors as the shadow of the gelim grew closer.

"The gelim?" came Sam's voice.

"It's here too."

I held my breath, waiting for the monster to crash through the glass, but when the doors opened, it wasn't the gelim that entered. It was Miss DeVore.

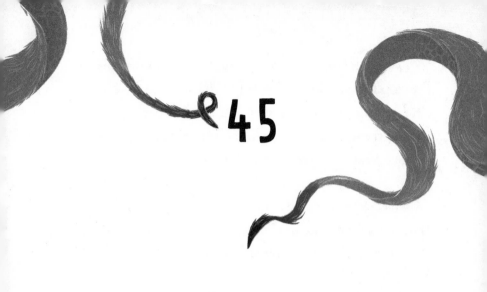

# 45

MISS DEVORE WAS wearing a plain blue dress, and her hair was fixed in a helmet of silver curls. Shadowless, she walked toward me, her lips pulled back in a smile to reveal lipstick-stained teeth. "Hector Griggs, you naughty boy."

I looked around for the others and spotted Sam with the boys from lunch at my regular table. Most of the students were eating and talking like their lives weren't in danger. Miss Musser, Mrs. Ford, and Mr. Grady were making their rounds, keeping the students in line. I didn't see Blake or Orson, and I hoped they were safe.

"Sorry to steal your dinner," I said, trying to sound braver than I felt.

Miss DeVore spread her hands. "You're a bit scrawny, but you'll make a fine enough meal once I strip the meat from your bones."

Despite having just sprinted under the punishing Florida sun, I felt cold and clammy as the sweat chilled on my skin. I needed to find a way to distract Miss DeVore so that I could try to make her visible to everyone in the cafeteria, but she kept her eyes on me and didn't blink. "What are you?"

Miss DeVore spread her arms wide. "This world is more than simply a destination for lost objects. It's a place of lost dreams *and* lost nightmares. There are things here you can't begin to imagine."

We circled each other, both of us looking for an advantage. "So you made a nest at the school and spent the last seventy years eating boys you thought no one would miss?"

"And it was so easy." Miss DeVore laughed like a hyena. "You're all terribly frightened of being different, afraid of being the one nobody wants to sit with at lunch. Helping you fall through the cracks to this world hardly took any effort on my part."

"You really are a monster."

"Who's the monster?" Miss DeVore asked. "You sweaty, smelly boys spend your years trying to prove you're the strongest in the pack. You call each other names, you fight, you pick at insecurities like scabs just to see if you can make each other bleed. Look at how easily I drove a wedge between you and your so-called best friend."

"Why did you tell me to fight for him, though?" I asked, recalling the conversation we had during detention.

"Because conflict is delicious, Hector," she said. "I

wanted you to keep trying because the savory flavor of your failure to win back your best friend paired so well with Orson Wellington's misery."

I glanced at my watch. Lunch would end soon. I was running out of time. "But you failed. Blake and I made up."

Miss DeVore shrugged. "For now. But there will come another time when he'll meet a group of boys he wants to impress or a girl he fancies, and he'll put you down to gain their favor."

I wanted to shout at her that Blake would never do that, but he'd already done it once. I wanted to yell that he'd learned to be better and wouldn't hurt me again, but I couldn't say that for sure. The truth was that Miss DeVore might be right. Blake and I might fight again. But this time I understood something she didn't.

"You used Blake to try to bully me into believing that who I am isn't good enough. But it is. I am." I puffed out my chest, trying to stand tall before Miss DeVore. "I didn't believe that before, but I believe it now. The way we talk about ourselves matters, because words can be weapons, but they can also be shields."

Miss DeVore paused to look at me thoughtfully. Warily. "You're different, you know? You're not like Orson and my other meals."

"You mean the boys you trapped in your nest?"

"I've been watching you since you transferred to St. Lawrence's, Hector. You're different. You belong *here*. Your ability to travel freely between worlds is exceptionally rare."

"Is that why you tried to lure me to the clergy house when Blake was chasing me?"

Miss DeVore smiled, revealing gray, crooked teeth. "It was a test. Only a special child such as yourself could have heard my voice without being over here." She paused and licked her lips. "Work with me instead of against me. We would be a formidable team."

A response leapt to my tongue, but a single thought held it back. Miss DeVore, the gelim, was afraid. Why else would she be talking to me instead of attacking? Why would she want to be my partner? If I really was as special as she said, and she wanted to use me, she wouldn't have asked. She would have forced me to do what she wanted. Which meant she couldn't compel me, and that scared her. *I* scared her.

"Think about it," Miss DeVore went on. "No one would call you names. No one would push you around or tell you what to do. You wouldn't have to endure bullies or bedtimes or brothers."

I want to say I wasn't tempted, but I remembered what it had been like the first time Blake called me that awful name. I'd felt powerless; I'd felt alone; I'd felt so worthless that I'd wanted to hide forever. And I never wanted anyone to be able to make me feel that ashamed again. Accepting the gelim's offer might have given me that security, but it would have taken away everything that made me who I was. I would have become the monster I was fighting.

"No thank you," I said.

Miss DeVore flinched and shook her head. "Then I

suppose we have nothing left to discuss." She held out her arms as her skin began to ripple and bubble.

The bell rang. Miss DeVore glanced over her shoulder as five hundred boys stood. In that moment, her attention wavered. I'd never get a better opportunity, so I launched myself at Miss DeVore and wrapped my arms around her waist. With every ounce of concentration, I begged the universe to make us visible.

I could feel the gelim resist. Fighting her was like swimming through pudding. She squirmed and thrashed, but I locked my hands together and refused to let go. Miss DeVore clawed at the air, attempting to remain anchored to her world, while I poured all my strength into dragging her into mine. It was a contest I wasn't sure I could win, but I wasn't going to quit until I had nothing left to give.

With a satisfying pop, like finally opening a stubborn lid on a new jar of jelly, we crossed over and crashed to the floor. Around us, students gasped. I looked up and found Miss Musser standing nearby, glaring at me and Miss DeVore.

"Hector Griggs, what in heaven's name do you think you're doing to poor Miss DeVore?"

Adults don't often see what's right in front of them if it doesn't fit their expectations. Miss Musser saw a student fighting an old lady. She didn't see the patches of Miss DeVore's skin that were green and scaly or that jagged teeth were growing out of her mouth or that her arms and legs were longer than was humanly possible.

But the other boys saw. Students cried out, "Gelim!" and "Monster!" Even though Sam, Blake, and I had only begun telling the story that morning, it had caught fire as easily as the clergy house.

Miss DeVore stood, slowly. She looked like a wax figure, melting, and even Miss Musser finally realized that *something* was wrong.

"She's a monster!" I shouted. "Miss DeVore's the gelim!"

"Now, Hector," began Miss Musser, but she was cut off when Miss DeVore exploded. Hundreds of tentacles burst free from the costume the gelim had worn for seventy years. The monster expanded. I'd never seen more than a couple of its tentacles at one time, and I wasn't prepared for the sight. A grotesque body like an infected wart covered with eyestalks and tentacles grew up and out until it brushed the ceiling. Its skin was green and bumpy like a toad, and it was dripping mucus. Its bulbous yellow eyes stared menacingly at us as it gnashed its gnarly teeth.

I turned to tell Miss Musser to run when a tentacle smacked me in the chest. As I hit the wall, all I heard were screams.

# 46

MY BODY HAD nearly reached the limit of abuse it could take in one day. From my thumbs to my pinkie toes, everything hurt. I felt pain in parts of my body I hadn't known could experience pain. As I tried to sit up, I grew dizzy and fell back. I focused on what was going on around me. Students were screaming and cowering under tables as the gelim's countless tentacles spread like vines across the floor and up the walls. The cafeteria was a buffet of terror for the gelim to feast on, and I'd rung the dinner bell.

"Hector!" Blake dashed toward me, followed by Orson, who was crawling through the chaos on his hands and knees. Blake dropped down onto the floor while he tried to catch his breath.

"Blake! Orson! What are you doing here?" I was surprised to see them.

"We got here . . . as soon . . . as we could." Orson didn't

look so good, and he could barely speak without a break between words.

"You should be somewhere safe."

Blake was holding a baseball bat in one hand, and he chucked me in the shoulder with the other. "That was a rotten trick you pulled in the attic, but we're here now. What do we do?"

I didn't know. I'd done my job: I'd gotten the gelim to the cafeteria. I had no idea what came next. "We should find Sam."

"Can't we just rest here?" Orson said.

Blake clapped him on the back. "Sorry, buddy." He pulled Orson's arm around his shoulders, and they followed me as I ducked and ran along the wall toward the kitchen. Everywhere the gelim's tentacles touched, greasy black mold spread.

I didn't see Sam, but I spotted Miss Musser and ran for her. She was barking orders to a group of students who had formed up around her. They were flipping over tables to form a barrier and using whatever they could find as weapons—frying pans, lunch trays, brooms, and mops. Miss Musser and her students fought the gelim, creating a distraction while Mrs. Ford organized the youngest students into small groups and led them toward the emergency exit at the back of the building.

I spotted Paul on the other side of the room, and tried to make my way to him, hoping he would know where Sam was. When I got there, he was with Matt and Trevor and a group of eighth-grade boys. They'd taken the lead from Miss Musser and set up their own barricade of tables and chairs, but the wall was barely holding the gelim back.

"Are you seeing this, Hector?" Paul had a nasty bruise across his cheek, and some of the other boys were sporting injuries too.

As I was about to answer, I heard a familiar voice.

"Grab whatever you can use as a weapon!"

"Jason?" When he didn't answer, I called his name again louder.

Jason's head popped up. He saw me and grinned. "You weren't kidding about the monster."

I hung my head. "Sorry."

"Sorry?" Jason said. "I haven't had this much fun at school ever."

I shouldn't have been surprised that Jason was enjoying himself. "What are you doing?"

Jason puffed out his chest. "Getting ready to attack."

I looked at Paul. "You guys too?"

Trevor scowled at me. "We can't run and hide."

Matt raised his hand. "That sounds like a good plan to me."

"You got good friends." Jason hiked his thumb at Paul. "Saved me from getting the life squeezed out of me."

Paul's cheeks turned red. "Just doing what any good cupcake would do."

I never expected to find Jason and his eighth-grade friends working with the boys from lunch, but it was that kind of day. "You should stay here where it's safe."

"Look around. Nowhere is safe."

Jason was right. The gelim was turning the cafeteria into a new nest to replace the one I'd burned down. There were pockets of students fighting back, but they were barely holding their ground.

"Jason . . ."

"Hey, that Sam kid was looking for you."

"Where?"

"By the bathrooms." Jason pointed toward the rear of the cafeteria.

I wondered if there was anything I could say to make Jason reconsider leading an assault on the gelim. "You don't have to do this, you know?"

"I owe it one," Jason said. "No one hits my brother but me."

Blake held out the bat to him. "You're going to need this."

Jason took the bat and responded with a short nod.

There were fewer tentacles the farther back we went, and I finally spied Sam sitting with Jackson. She had her walkie-talkie out and was calling into it. As soon as she saw me, she threw herself at me and hugged me like she hadn't seen me in days. When she was finished, I slid to the floor, unable to stand any longer, while she hugged Orson and Blake.

"I'm so glad you're alive!" Sam said, and I was a little

worried that she'd thought I might not be, but I had more important concerns.

"We got the gelim here. What now? You said you had a plan, right?"

Sam nodded. "Help is on the way."

"Soon?" Jackson said. There was blood on his shirt from a nasty gash on his forehead.

Orson looked worried. "What if it disappears before then? We'll never get another chance like this."

All around us, students and teachers were fighting back against the gelim, even gaining ground in some places, but Orson was right. The gelim could shift to its world if we didn't stop it, and then everything we'd accomplished would be for nothing. Luckily, I had an idea. I wasn't sure it would work, but I was determined to try. "Help me?" Blake pulled my arm around his shoulders so I could take some weight off my ankle. "I need to get to the gelim. I'm going to trap it here the same way it traps boys in its world."

"Not a chance!" Sam said. "It's too dangerous."

She wasn't wrong, but I said, "There's no other way."

Orson held up his hands. "I can't. I can't go near that thing again."

I understood. "You don't have to." I turned to Blake. "Neither do you."

Blake laughed. "Friends for life, right?"

Everyone who wasn't helping the younger boys flee was fighting. Even Coach Barbary was there. I didn't know where he'd come from, but he was swinging an aluminum baseball bat like a cudgel, carving a path through the tentacles.

"That way." I pointed toward Coach.

With Blake's help, I limped through the carnage. Boys who saw me called my name and cheered. Jason spied me from where he was fighting. He had green goo in his hair and splattered across his arms. He held his fist in the air and grinned before a wave of tentacles crashed into him. Jackson took over supporting me so that Blake could help Sam beat a path through the chaos.

"We have to get as close to the center as possible," I said. I felt the gelim's fear. But it wasn't only fear. It was desperation. It was disbelief that a group of children could defeat it. The monster had spent decades feeding off the boys it thought no one would miss, and now those boys were fighting back.

The gelim had only preyed on us when we were alone. It had no idea how strong we were when we stood together.

Sam, Blake, Jackson, and I got as close as we could to the pulsating mass of the gelim. I braced myself against its body, ignoring the stench. I made myself an anchor. I wasn't going anywhere, and neither was the gelim.

The monster shuddered when it realized my plan. It was trying to slip away. To run. But it couldn't escape. I wouldn't let it.

*You're a* freak, Hector! The gelim's voice sounded in my head. In all our heads. *You'll always be a* freak!

It was trying to shake me loose.

"No he's not!" Blake yelled.

*Even if you win today, you'll still be a loser.*

But that wasn't true either. Because even if we lost this battle and the gelim got away, we'd already won by showing up and fighting for what was right.

The gelim bucked and thrashed. A tentacle curled in and reached for me, but Blake slashed at it with his pocket-knife. Gray blood spurted from the wound.

*You can't do this forever, Hector! You're not strong enough!*

That was one thing the monster was right about. I didn't know how long I could hold on. A tentacle slithered in and wrapped around my ankle. It pulled, trying to dislodge me. I was losing my grip.

"Yaaaaargh!" Orson Wellington charged toward me, holding a pair of scissors over his head, and stabbed them into the tentacle around my leg. The blades tore into the meat, and the gelim shrieked in pain and released me. Orson slipped in the blood that sprayed from the wound, but Sam caught him before he fell. Together Blake, Sam, Jackson, and Orson formed a circle around me.

The gelim was right. I wasn't strong enough. But I didn't need to be. Because together, *we* were strong enough. We were all strong and all worthy. Me, Sam, Blake, and Orson. The cupcakes, Gordi and Evan, Jason. Our teachers: Miss Musser, who wasn't a colonel but fought like a soldier; Coach Barbary, who I suspected had encountered this monster before; and even Mrs. Ford, who wasn't fighting but hadn't run away, either. With the strength of the entire school behind me, I could hold the gelim right where it was as long as I needed to.

The cafeteria doors burst open. A group of people in hazmat suits surged in, armed with weapons that looked like cattle prods. The gelim's fear was palpable as it finally realized it had lost, and I almost felt sorry for it.

Almost.

"Help is here," Sam said, sounding exhausted and relieved.

"Finally!" Orson wailed.

At the tail end of the squad walked Mr. Morhill, in a sharp black suit. "Great job, everyone," he said, "but we'll take it from here."

## 47

A NICE PARAMEDIC with bright red hair and a brighter smile finished taping gauze over the scrapes on my elbow before letting me go. Fire trucks and ambulances and police cars had arrived shortly after Mr. Morhill had shown up with his army of agents. Mr. Morhill's people had sealed off the cafeteria, and no one else was allowed inside.

Blake was hanging out with Paul, Trevor, Jackson, Matt, Gordi, and Evan. There were a lot of cuts and bruises, but no one had been seriously injured. Blake's eyes lit up when he spotted me.

"Get this! They're saying it was some kind of toxic fumes and that we all hallucinated what happened!" Blake busted up laughing, and the other boys joined in.

"No one's going to buy that story," Gordi said. "Right?"

Paul shook his head. "Adults will. They're so gullible.

They'll believe anything if it means not having to admit there was a monster working in the principal's office."

I couldn't believe we'd actually won. We'd beaten the gelim. I stood with the boys for a while, listening to them tell their parts of what had happened. Everyone, it seemed, had played a role in our victory. The boys from my lunch table were still cupcakes, but now they wore the name like a badge of honor. They'd reclaimed it, and no one could use it to hurt them again.

I spotted Coach Barbary leaning against a tree, standing quietly alone, and jogged over to him.

"Toxic fumes, huh?" Coach said.

"That's what they're saying." I dug into my pocket and pulled out the watch I'd found in the attic of the clergy house. I handed it to Coach.

"What's this?" He rubbed his thumb over the face before turning it over. When he read the name on the back, tears welled in his eyes. "I never stopped wondering what happened to him. I even came back to teach here because I hoped, one day, maybe I'd figure it out."

"Is that why you gave me the key to the clergy house?"

Coach nodded. "I knew that there was something wrong at this school, though not exactly what, and that the clergy house was at the center. I wish I could have helped you more."

"He must have been a really good friend if you never forgot about him." As sad as it was, it gave me hope that there were people out there who remembered all the boys who'd been lost over the years. It wouldn't bring them back, but at least they might not be totally forgotten.

"He was the best friend I ever had." Coach Barbary lowered his head.

"I'm sorry for your loss." I didn't know what else to say, so I left Coach alone with the watch and his thoughts.

I passed Jason, who was surrounded by a group of boys from every grade congratulating him and cheering for him. He was a hero today. He caught my eye and smiled. Maybe we weren't ever going to be friends, but we'd always be brothers.

Miss Musser snagged my arm as I walked past. "It seems I owe you an apology, Hector Griggs." She had a bruise across her face, but she seemed otherwise unhurt.

"For what?"

"I don't know how any of this is possible or even what really happened, but you clearly weren't telling stories the day you claimed you'd seen a monster, were you?"

I shrugged. "Maybe there are toxic fumes in the main building too."

Miss Musser snorted. "Right."

Though it might have been a small matter compared to everything else we'd been through, there was something I needed to get off my chest. "Miss Musser?"

"Yes, Hector?"

"Blake wasn't lying either. About his science project, I mean. I set it on fire."

Miss Musser's right eyebrow arched so high it nearly

disappeared into her hair. "Why on earth would you do something that reckless?"

"I know. I thought I had a good reason for doing it, but I didn't. It was wrong."

Miss Musser stared at me with disappointment, which I'd earned. Finally, she said, "Well, I've already allowed Blake to redo his project, but I penalized him a full letter grade for turning it in late. In light of what you've told me, I'm taking a letter grade from your project and giving it to Blake."

"That sounds fair." A letter grade was a small price to pay for surviving a fight with a monster, getting my best friend back, and making a whole bunch of new friends.

Miss Musser pursed her lips. "Go on. Before I change my mind."

I took off through the crowd of students and teachers. Everyone seemed to know I'd had something to do with what we'd just been through, but no one was sure exactly what role I'd played. One thing was certain, though: I wasn't invisible.

While I was looking for Sam so I could finally get some answers, I found Orson sitting alone on the sidewalk watching the agents in hazmat suits scurry into and out of the cafeteria. Everything hurt as I lowered myself down beside him.

"What do you think's going to happen to me?" Orson asked.

"What do you mean?"

"Do you think people will remember me now?"

"After what you did today," I said, "I don't think anyone will ever forget you."

"What about my folks?"

I didn't know the answer. Orson had been lost for three years. He hadn't aged a day. His parents hadn't noticed he was missing. Would they remember him like no time had passed or would they suddenly feel the weight of those missing three years?

"Guess we'll find out together," I said.

"I'm scared."

I hung my arm over Orson's shoulders. "That's okay. Not knowing what's going to happen is scary."

"Yeah."

"You were afraid of the gelim, too, but you kicked its butt."

"Not alone," he said.

"You're not alone now, either."

Parents had already begun arriving. The police tried to organize a barrier for them to wait behind, but nothing could stop the horde of concerned parents from reaching their children.

I was about to go hunt for Sam again when Orson rose slowly to his feet. I followed his gaze and spotted two adults who looked like they were seeing a ghost. Both were sobbing.

"Mom?" Orson said. "Dad?"

Mrs. Wellington wailed, "Orson!" and ran toward him,

nearly bowling him over when they met. Orson's parents wrapped him in a tearful, joyful hug. I guess they hadn't completely forgotten about him after all.

My own reunion with Mom and Pop was no less emotional. Pop broke into tears when he found me and Jason, and he sank to his knees on the asphalt to hug us both. When he finally let go, he led us to the squad car, where Mom was waiting with more hugs. Even though it hurt a little after everything I'd been through, I didn't complain. Jason tried to tell Mom and Pop the story of what really happened in the cafeteria, but I wasn't sure they believed him. If I hadn't been there, *I* wouldn't have believed it. Maybe they assumed his story was the product of "toxic fumes." Or maybe they were too happy we were safe to care.

"It was so cool," Jason said. "But Hector's the real hero. We'd all be dead if it weren't for him."

Pop said, "You know? I'm not surprised. He takes after his mom that way."

"Well, whatever happened today," Mom said, "I think you boys deserve a treat. What'll it be?"

Before I could make a suggestion, Jason said, "How about lemon meringue pie for Hector?"

I stared at him, my mouth open. "Really?"

Mom and Pop glanced at each other and smiled. "Anything you want," Mom said.

Jason leaned over and whispered, "You're still a pianist."

I could live with that.

# 48

SCHOOL REMAINED CLOSED, giving students a couple of unexpected days off. Just like Paul had predicted, the adults had gobbled up the story about the toxic fumes—even most of the teachers who'd been in the cafeteria and had seen Miss DeVore turn into the gelim. It was probably for the best.

Mom and Pop were letting me have my friends over for a sleepover on Saturday. I was surprised when Mom called me from my room and told me there was a girl at the door to see me.

"She looks familiar," Mom said. "Have I met her before?"

I shrugged, unsure what to say.

"How do you know her?"

"From around the neighborhood. She's not here for the sleepover." I took off to keep Mom from asking more questions.

Sam was sitting on her bicycle in the driveway. She didn't look any different to me, so I wasn't sure why Mom hadn't recognized her, but that was just one of the many, *many* mysteries of Sam Osborne.

"Hey," she said.

"Hey."

Sam got off her bike and set it down in the grass. "How are you feeling?"

I shrugged. "Still a little sore, but okay."

"Good."

"You?"

"I'm fine."

"You talk to Orson?" I asked.

"Yesterday," she said. "You know he already looks three years older? Like he grew up overnight. His family has convinced themselves that he was kidnapped this whole time."

"Weird." I felt bad that Orson had lost those three years, but at the same time, I doubted he would have wanted to spend another day stuck being twelve. It also meant he would probably head off to high school and I wouldn't see him again.

Sam and I stood across from each other. I had my hands folded over my chest, she had hers stuffed in her pockets.

"I found out what *gelim* means," Sam said.

I looked at her questioningly. "And?"

"It's an Old Irish word meaning 'I consume' or 'I devour.'"

Even if gelim wasn't the monster's true name, it was still a pretty spot-on description. I wondered which of the boys that the gelim had fed on had come up with it. Sadly, I doubted I would ever know.

"Have you tried turning invisible since the other day?" Sam asked.

I shook my head. "Not sure I want to."

"It could be useful."

"And dangerous."

"Maybe," Sam said. "But even if there are more monsters like the gelim, I don't think any of them will be able to trap you there again."

"Are you sure?"

"Pretty much. Yeah."

"So . . . are you going to tell me who Mr. Morhill really works for? Is he even your uncle? What or who is Kairos?"

Sam sighed and sat down, pulling her knees to her chest. "Kairos is an organization that Uncle Archie works for. And he isn't actually my uncle, but he may as well be. Officially, he's my guardian."

"Okay, but what kind of organization is Kairos?"

"The secret kind." Sam paused a moment before continuing. "Kairos has been around for centuries. The world is full of strange creatures, people with amazing abilities, and things I can't even describe. Kairos investigates them, helps out when we can, and prevents them from causing harm when necessary."

A few things clicked into place. "Miss Calloway didn't win the lottery, did she?"

"She did," Sam said. "But only because Kairos arranged it."

"And you and Mr. Morhill came here to investigate the gelim?"

"We didn't know what we were going to find when we arrived. Kairos heard rumors there was a ghost at St. Lawrence's and sent Uncle Archie to check it out. He didn't bring me in until you told him you'd heard the ghost. He had a feeling you weren't telling him everything and thought you might trust me more than him."

I wasn't sure if I should be upset that they'd lied to me. "So you work for this Kairos organization too?"

Sam nodded. "Kairos is always looking for young people like us who have unique abilities that can help them."

"Us?"

"I can make people see me as whatever I want them to see. That's how I was able to blend in at St. Lawrence's even though I'm not a boy."

"You didn't look any different to me."

"I think it's because you're special."

"Because I can travel to the place where lost things go?"

"Not exactly," Sam said. "You were able to hear the gelim whisper to you when you weren't in the other world. I think you could hear it and see through my disguise because you're sensitive."

*Sensitive.* It didn't sound bad when Sam said it. It sounded like a gift rather than a curse.

"Maybe it's connected to your ability to travel," Sam was saying, "but it might just be part of who you are."

This was a lot to digest. Sam *and* Mr. Morhill were part

of a secret organization, Sam had powers, *I* had powers, and there were possibly more terrifying things in the universe than the gelim.

"I still can't believe the gelim was Miss DeVore."

Sam nodded. "But it was perfect. As Principal O'Shea's secretary, she saw the boys who wound up in his office. She knew which boys were bullies, and which ones were being bullied, and since she took care of the student files, she made sure no one noticed that students were going missing."

"Was there ever a real Miss DeVore?"

"Probably," Sam said. "I don't think the gelim could travel between worlds like you. We think it would have needed a connection to a person in our world first." She shook her head. "There's still so much about the gelim we don't know."

"What about Conrad?"

Sam bowed her head. "There *was* a Conrad Eldridge. Agents found his file stuffed behind a drawer in Miss DeVore's desk when they searched it." She must've seen the look on my face because she quickly added, "It wasn't actually him. The real Conrad had been gone for years. There was nothing we could've done to save him."

I thought about how close Blake had come to winding up like Conrad. "What's going to happen to the gelim? Kairos won't hurt it, will they?" Even though it would have tried to eat me, I didn't like the idea of Kairos killing it. Just because it was a monster didn't mean it deserved to die.

"It's alive," Sam said. "But I don't know more than that."

"Oh." A thought occurred to me. "So, now that the gelim's gone, does that mean Mr. Morhill will be leaving?"

Sam nodded.

"You too?"

"We've got other 'ghosts' to investigate." Sam looked over at me and caught my eye. "That's one of the reasons I'm here. With your gift, you'd be a huge asset to Kairos. Even if you don't want to work in the field, they'd like to study what you can do and how you do it."

"You want me to join Kairos?"

"Look at how much good you did at your school," Sam said. "You rescued Orson. You saved Blake. If you hadn't exposed Miss DeVore, the gelim would have continued feeding on students. You're a hero, Hector."

But I didn't feel like a hero. I couldn't stop thinking about the boys I hadn't been able to help. "I don't know. Things are good here. Even Pop treats me differently. He moved the piano into the living room and told Jason if he didn't stop complaining about it, he'd make him take lessons too."

Sam laughed. "I get it. But there's a whole world where lost things go, and you might be the only person alive who can explore it."

Sam made it sound like an adventure, and her offer *was* tempting. "Can I think about it?"

"Of course. You can call me anytime, even if you decide not to join and you just want to talk." Sam stood and brushed off her hands on her shorts. "Just promise me if you do use your power, you'll be careful. We don't know anything about what's over there, and I don't want to have to save your butt again."

I snorted and laughed. "I will."

Sam threw her arms around my neck and hugged me. "I'm glad I got to know you, Hector Griggs."

I hugged her back, and even though it felt like goodbye, I suspected this wouldn't be the last time we saw each other.

I stood in the driveway until Sam had biked away. Mom was waiting for me inside. "You didn't want to invite her to stay? Blake and your other friends will be here soon."

"She had other things to do." I wondered where Sam and Mr. Morhill would be off to next. Another ghost at a different school? A monster at a summer camp? I supposed the only way to know was to join Kairos, but I'd spent enough time being invisible for a while. Right now, I just wanted to be seen.

**To:** Kairos Director
**From:** Samantha Osborne
**Subject:** Hector Griggs

I did my best to convince Hector to join Kairos, but between other worlds and tentacle monsters trying to eat him, he's a little overwhelmed. I recommend giving Hector space and letting him come to us.

And if he never does, well, he can't possibly be the only person who can travel between our world and the place where lost things go. We'll find someone else.

—*Sam*

**To:** Agent Strix
**From:** Kairos Director
**Subject:** Asset H.G.

Maintain surveillance on H.G. If he cannot be recruited before the next phase, he will need to be eliminated.

# ACKNOWLEDGMENTS

I've had this story in my head in various forms for at least a decade, and I'm not sure I would have had the skill or courage to write it without the help of a lot of folks.

Katie Shea Boutillier for quietly nudging me throughout the years about that middle-grade novel I kept talking about, and for helping me carve out some space to write it.

Liesa Abrams for inviting me to be part of the Labyrinth Road family, for helping me find the best way to tell the story I knew was buried in the jumble of pages I turned in, and for gently guiding me as I fumbled through unfamiliar terrain.

Emily Harburg for falling in love with these characters and helping me unravel the twisty plot logic.

Everyone behind the scenes at Labyrinth Road and Penguin Random House who helped bring this book to life: Carol Ly, Jen Valero, Rebecca Vitkus, Barbara Bakowski, and so many more. Your contributions are immeasurable, and though it must often feel like thankless work, I am forever grateful.

Cookie Hiponia for Picard nights and the long, rambling

phone calls that helped me bring so much of this story into focus.

My family for being there always.

*The School for Invisible Boys* also owes a great debt to Madeline L'Engle and John Bellairs, whose books inspired me as a child and continue to inspire me as an adult.

Lastly, I'd like to thank the librarians and teachers who continue to fight for the rights of all children to be seen, often at great risk to their careers and safety. I didn't appreciate what those special teachers and librarians did for me when I was younger, but the difference they made in my life was incalculable, as is the difference you're making in the lives of children today. My books wouldn't exist without your kindness, tenacity, and courage.